Dear Reader,

When I wrote *Captivated,* I was a young mother juggling the joys and demands of a career, a small daughter (with a son on the way!) and a house that needed work. A lot of work. Some of my best plots came to me with paintbrush in hand!

I've been a journalist and a musician, but my first love has always been writing novels. Growing up in rural New England, I'd climb a tree with pad and pen or sit on a rock in the middle of the brook on our "farm" and spin stories. For me, selling my first books at such a young age is a dream come true.

I've never been a writer who chains herself to a desk. I've always had a zest for adventure that shows up both in my "real life" and the stories I create. I think you'll see that here, in *Captivated,* with Sheridan Weaver and Richard St. Charles.

I'm hard at work on my next book and so fortunate to be able to keep doing what I love, thanks to readers like you.

Many thanks to Harlequin for publishing *Captivated,* and happy 60th birthday!

Take care,

Carla Neggers

THE HARLEQUIN FAMOUS FIRSTS COLLECTION™

NEW YORK TIMES BESTSELLING AUTHOR

CARLA NEGGERS

CAPTIVATED

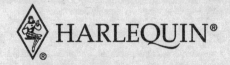

HARLEQUIN®

TORONTO • NEW YORK • LONDON
AMSTERDAM • PARIS • SYDNEY • HAMBURG
STOCKHOLM • ATHENS • TOKYO • MILAN • MADRID
PRAGUE • WARSAW • BUDAPEST • AUCKLAND

Recycling programs
for this product may
not exist in your area.

ISBN-13: 978-0-373-20010-8

CAPTIVATED

www.eHarlequin.com

Printed in U.S.A.

1

"AGNEW," SHERIDAN WEAVER said, plunking down the printout she was going through, "it's bad enough that I have to spend my lunch hour working on the Johnson report. I don't need you breathing down my neck. Go lust after someone else's window."

All in all Sheridan thought her rebuff good-humored. Donald Agnew, the major reason the Johnson report was late, would understand. Not that it mattered if he did since he reported to Sheridan, a senior financial analyst with United Commercial Insurance in Boston. She and Agnew got along all right and understood each other. He wanted Sheridan's job, which she didn't mind and considered a good attitude on his part. But he would have settled for her cubby by the window. This she did mind. She had an impressive view of the city and, across the harbor, Logan Airport. Agnew had an irritating habit of coming by and staring dreamy eyed out her window. On a warm, clear day in May, like today, he could imagine he was going to Paris. Sheridan had already been to Paris. She was also not given to daydreaming. Throughout United Commercial, Sheridan Weaver was known as a woman with both feet flat on the floor. She knew it...and approved.

When the shadow remained stubbornly over the page she was trying to read, she sighed. "You're in my light."

"Sorry."

That was not Agnew's voice and certainly not something Agnew would have said. He was never so simple or so direct. He would have said, "And here I thought I was your light, Sher." He liked to think he was witty. Sheridan had worked with worse.

Finally she looked up at the man leaning against the divider to her cubby. Her eyes widened. "You're not Agnew."

The man said without smiling, "No."

Whereas Agnew was lanky, almost skinny, her visitor was solid and muscular and topped by six inches the United Commercial calendar hanging on the divider. Agnew came to the steeple of the New England church in the May photograph. And Agnew dressed conservatively during his hours at U. C., usually in clothes much too rich for his budget. He was a true Yuppie. This man, however, wore a classy eye-catching combination of pleated pants, an unstructured linen jacket and a T-shirt. He looked as if he could afford to wear anything he chose. He had a straight, regal nose, an arrogant turn to his full mouth and hair that was thick and very dark, offset by black eyebrows and large black eyes.

As far as Sheridan could see, he didn't belong on the thirtieth floor of the United Commercial Insurance Building.

She reminded herself she was a responsible member

of the management team of the international insurance firm…and decided to act like one. "May I help you?"

"You're Sheridan Weaver?"

He had a deep, quiet voice, but it was rough at the edges and noticeably confident. Involuntarily Sheridan pushed back a few strands of her own dark hair, aware not only of him but of herself, too, and what he must be thinking of her. But who was he? Not Floyd Johnson, she hoped. No, no, that was impossible. Anyone who made her do a useless report like the one she was slaving over wouldn't wear T-shirts.

No executive within fifty miles of Boston would wear a T-shirt.

"Yes, I'm Sheridan Weaver." Her voice was steady, but her stomach was not. She liked order in her life. She didn't like surprises. Especially surprises that were distinctly male and distinctly inappropriate for the office.

"My name is Richard St. Charles," he said and paused, as if expecting a reaction. He received none. Sheridan had never heard of Richard St. Charles.

"I'm from San Francisco," he went on. "I would like to talk to you in private—elsewhere."

"Why? What's this about?"

"It's about your father."

She tensed, her entire body going rigid at his words. "My father? Is he all right? He isn't—"

"Then your father is J.B. Weaver, the San Francisco private investigator? Jorgensen Beaumont Weaver?"

There could be only one. Sheridan nodded dully. She was no longer thinking about Richard St. Charles's impressive voice or his T-shirt. J. B. had never contacted her at work before. Never. Something had to be wrong.

Richard St. Charles went on in that mild, captivating tone. "I understood he was here in Boston visiting you."

The tension in her body was released just as suddenly as it had manifested itself. She sagged, her hands trembling, and erupted with something between a laugh and a sob. "Thank God," she mumbled. "I thought he'd been hurt."

The man moved, just a fraction of an inch, but he had the kind of body and presence that made even the slightest movement noticeable. "Then obviously he's not here with you."

Sheridan winced; now she'd done it. J. B. had a bothersome habit of leaving word with his secretary to tell anyone he didn't want to see—police detectives, district attorneys, lawyers, rival investigators, clients, thugs—that he was visiting his daughter in Boston. Even more irksome, he never gave Sheridan any advance warning. Irate people would call her at all hours of the night.

But never had one actually come to Boston and tracked her down. She wondered who Richard St. Charles was and how much trouble she'd just gotten her father into by not stonewalling for him.

"Are you a client?" she asked hopefully.

His face remained impassive. "No."

Sheridan chewed on the corner of her mouth. It was parched; the rest of her was drenched. She could feel the perspiration soaking into her white pinpoint oxford blouse. Her colleagues at U. C. didn't know about J.B.

Weaver. He belonged to another life, was the father of another Sheridan Weaver. This Sheridan Weaver had an MBA and wore pale-gray *structured* linen suits and black pumps to work. She kept her nails manicured and polished in neutral colors and her thick dark hair knotted at the back of her head. She wore pearl earrings and dull cosmetics. She was successful, competent, dutiful and proper.

That other Sheridan Weaver was brash, daring and devil-may-care. She was also, like her father, a licensed private investigator. Before coming to Boston a year ago, she had been J.B. Weaver's renowned, cocky and very capable partner.

It had been the two of them for so long that Sheridan couldn't begin to guess what J. B. had taught her and what she had learned by osmosis, just from being around him and his work all her life. When he had agreed to make her his partner, not an associate but a full-fledged partner, she had been thrilled. That had been the culmination of all her dreams. Then one day she asked herself if maybe it had been the culmination of all *J. B.'s* dreams. She wasn't sure of the answer. But she had to find out.

Breaking away from that world had been difficult for both father and daughter, though J. B. had insisted he understood: Sheridan needed to find out what the world was like outside the doors of a private investigator's office. When she found out, she'd be back, he was sure. Better and stronger, but still the daughter he knew. He'd given her six months, tops. He and his poker buddies had a pool, a wager on the day she'd dust off her license and resume her place at Weaver Investigations.

Almost a year had passed, and Sheridan was still working in Boston. Happily. The days of sharing J. B.'s office and coming up with new and often outrageous schemes to gather necessary information for their investigations were over—at least as far as she was concerned. She wasn't so sure about J. B. He had been making noises about getting her back to San Francisco by hook or by crook. Knowing her father, that could mean anything.

Including a tall dark-haired man in a T-shirt who was still staring at her impassively.

"I feel my ulcer acting up," she said.

Richard St. Charles didn't appear to care one way or the other. "I need only ten minutes of your time, Ms Weaver. Perhaps we could go for coffee."

She glanced around, checking for eavesdroppers, but saw no one. Explaining this striking individual to goggle-eyed secretaries and account executives and any other female who worked at United Commercial was going to be a heroic task, but, she knew, inevitable. He couldn't possibly have arrived at her cubby without being observed. She didn't, however, want to have to explain their conversation. As much as she loathed doing so, she would make up a lie. "He's my accountant," she'd tell them. No, that would never do. She'd think of something.

She gave him a look. "Are you from the police, Mr. St. Charles?" she asked archly.

"Ms Weaver—"

"The district attorney's office?"

He just looked at her, and she sighed. If only she had said in the first place, "J. B. who?" Or, "Of course, my father. Yes, he stayed here overnight, but now he's on his way to Iceland. He left this morning."

"I suppose it doesn't matter who you are," she said in a businesslike tone. "I'm not going off with you, for coffee or anything else, so you can forget that. If you want to talk to me, talk."

He straightened up, and she realized she'd been mistaken: he topped the calendar by a half foot. She herself was fairly tall—up to the bicycle leaning against the church, or five-foot-seven. He had eight inches on her. "I don't believe you'll want anyone to overhear what I have to say."

The man was stubborn, but that almost got Sheridan to relent. "I have a report to finish," she said tartly. "As it is, people are going to ask about you. What would they say if I went waltzing off with you in the middle of the day? I'm sorry, Mr. St. Charles, but I have a reputation to maintain."

"You're stonewalling, Ms Weaver."

Yes, that was true, but she didn't find his astuteness the least bit endearing. "I'm a cautious person. I don't go off with strangers—especially ones looking for my father. Now good day."

"Ms Weaver, you have nothing to fear from me."

"Are you implying other people do? Like my father perhaps?"

His eyes flickered, but with what she couldn't guess.

Annoyance? Interest? Surprise? "I'll take you to lunch," he suggested in a tone that indicated he wasn't accustomed to refusal. "We'll talk."

"No."

She went back to her printouts; he remained where he was. Clearly he expected his will to outmuscle hers, his stubbornness to outlast hers. This, she thought, was a grievous mistake on his part. She could be neither outmuscled nor outlasted. She was nothing if not tenacious, and long ago she had learned how to defend herself. J. B. had seen to that. He'd taught her everything about guns and fast-talking one's way out of a jam, as well as paying for her first judo and karate lessons.

But escorting Richard St. Charles out by his ear, although undoubtedly satisfying, would draw considerably more attention than merely having lunch with him.

She stuck a pencil into her electric sharpener, pulled it out and blew the dust off; it hadn't needed sharpening. "If you see J. B., give him my best."

He didn't make a sound, and when Sheridan finally looked up, he was gone. She counted to sixty before she grabbed her pencil and broke it in half. Her knees had been tensed in one position for so long that they buckled slightly when she got up, yet she didn't stumble as she made her way down the hall to the women's bathroom. She wanted to bang on the wall for a while, then wipe her hot face with cold wet paper towels, but two secretaries were there, smoking cigarettes and gossiping.

"Hey, Sheridan, who was that guy looking for you?"

"My accountant."

"No kidding? Wouldn't mind him doing my taxes."

People will believe anything, Sheridan thought, dashing into a stall.

Calming down wasn't easy. J. B. was a damned good detective, and she adored him for being the man and the father he was. But he was stubborn. He'd actually liked the idea of his daughter studying part-time to get her business degree, and even the thought of her spending her hiatus from detecting working for United Commercial in Boston had tickled him. But when the hiatus had gone beyond six months and showed signs of being permanent, J. B. had opened his mouth. In no uncertain terms, he told Sheridan she didn't belong in a cubbyhole office with a bottle of Maalox in her desk and an endless stack of printouts to read.

And in equally uncertain terms she'd told him she was out of the investigative business. When he had dropped none-too-vague hints about clients and cases, trying to whet what he considered her natural appetite for the business, she had decided enough was enough. "Just leave me out of it. I'm not your sidekick anymore!"

She was a sharp, businesslike financial analyst, and she liked her life. That was just something J. B. would have to get used to. And if he'd sent this Richard St. Charles as part of some new offensive to lure her back to the streets of San Francisco...

But what if he hadn't? What if this time J. B. really *was* in trouble? What if this time he really did need her?

"Don't worry, kid," he had always said; "when I need your help, I'll let you know."

Maybe Richard St. Charles was his way of letting her know. Or maybe J. B. wasn't in a position to contact her.

Sheridan washed her hands and practically ripped the towel container off the wall when she pulled out a paper towel. How was she going to get any work done? How was she going to get St. Charles and J. B. off her mind?

She stormed back to her cubby, where the Johnson report lay unfinished. Donald Agnew wandered by in his impeccable three-piece suit. "Noticed you had a visitor."

"Mmm." She tried to sound nonchalant. "A family friend." The accountant line would never work with Donald. "On the Johnson report—"

"I liked his clothes. Pretty cool." He grinned knowingly. "Must be quite a family friend if he took the trouble to come all the way up here."

Sheridan plopped down in her chair. "Agnew, don't be a jerk." She attacked the latest stack of printouts from data processing, but stopped suddenly, shooting a look up at her colleague. "Wait a minute! Agnew, say that again."

"What? Listen, Crabby, I was just suggesting a man who would take the trouble to look you up at work—"

"That's it!"

"Huh?"

"How did Richard St. Charles know I work at U. C.? My father always leaves word he's visiting his daughter in Boston. He never mentions where I work." She laughed, delighted with herself. "Ha, that's it!"

"Sher, you know something? You're nuts."

"Yeah, well, you should meet my father. No, forget I said that. Anyway, mystery solved."

Agnew pulled up a chair and sat down, all ears. "What mystery?"

Sheridan had already said too much and refused to incriminate herself further. Obviously Richard St. Charles was indeed a focal point in one of J.B. Weaver's plots to get Sheridan to see the error of her ways. St. Charles wouldn't know Sheridan worked at United Commercial unless J. B. had told him, and J. B. wouldn't have told him unless he and St. Charles were friends. Knowing J. B., they were colleagues, and the whole silly scheme had been concocted during a Thursday night poker game. Yes, she could see St. Charles as a San Francisco private investigator. Definitely. He had to be new in town; otherwise, she would have known him. But that would be why J. B. had chosen him.

"Well, case closed," she said and got back to work.

FIVE MINUTES BEFORE Sheridan and Agnew were to present the Johnson report, Richard St. Charles called. "Aren't you even the least bit curious about why I'd come this far to find your father?"

Sheridan glanced at Agnew, who was looking out her window and pretending to glance over the final report. "No," she said.

"You don't strike me as the kind of woman J.B. Weaver would have as a daughter."

"How perceptive of you."

He laughed softly and unexpectedly, with the same

subtle roughness that distinguished his voice. "Then you have none of his investigative talents?"

"Nary a one." Of course, if he were one of J. B.'s poker buddies, he would know she was lying.

"I see. Ms Weaver, obviously your father's secretary was lying when she told me I'd find him here. But that doesn't change anything. I still need to locate him."

"You're very good, Mr. St. Charles. Quite convincing. Even if I believed you were looking for my father, which I don't, I wouldn't tell you where he is—not, you understand, that I do know where he is."

"I beg your pardon?"

He sounded confused, which pleased her. "Never mind. Just go back to San Francisco and tell J. B. it didn't work, okay? I'm very happy being a financial analyst." Agnew hadn't turned a page in the past ten seconds. Sheridan turned her back to him and lowered her voice. "I'm due in a meeting."

She prepared to hang up, but his voice stopped her. Its roughness was much more apparent, but he nevertheless spoke quietly. "Ms Weaver, sooner or later your father is going to surface and get in touch with you. When he does, I'll be there."

"Look, don't you think you're carrying this a bit far?" There was an edge to her voice, too, but one of panic more than anger. What if maybe—just maybe—she had jumped to the wrong conclusion and Richard St. Charles was no friend of J.B. Weaver? And, therefore, no friend of hers?

"I mean what I say, Ms Weaver. I intend to find your father, with or without your help."

"Is that a threat, Mr. St. Charles? Because if it is— dammit, I don't have to listen to this!"

And she realized, *that's right, I don't.* She gave a nasty little chuckle and hung up. Hard.

Agnew winked. "Boy troubles, Sher?"

Donald Agnew had just given her reason to reveal her black-belt status in karate, but she managed to re- sist the impulse to kick him. "We're late," she said, snatched the report out of his hands and stalked off.

"Touchy, touchy," Agnew said, not in the least per- turbed.

SHERIDAN PRIDED HERSELF on being competent, profes- sional, sophisticated and in charge of her thoughts, but as she stumbled into her apartment building on Marl- borough Street in Boston's Back Bay at 6:05 P.M., she felt none of these. Her mind had wandered during the pre- sentation of the Johnson report. Her mind had wan- dered during a staff meeting after the presentation. Her mind had wandered while she sat at her desk, trying vainly to work.

And each time it had wandered to Richard St. Charles and his business in Boston. She couldn't shake him. He was there in her thoughts, with his black eyes and deep, quiet voice and eclectic clothes, with his ques- tions and his subtle threat: J. B. would get in touch with her, and St. Charles would be there when he did.

Or so he had said. Sheridan didn't believe him for a moment.

She sighed, digging out the key to her mailbox. But what if he *were* serious? J. B. had enemies. That was no secret and certainly no surprise. Private investigators made enemies just by doing their job well. Was St. Charles an enemy?

I'm going nuts, she thought, groaning in frustration at her ambivalence. If J. B. were crying wolf again, she didn't want to give him the satisfaction of following up on Mr. Richard St. Charles herself. But if J. B. were for real this time and if St. Charles weren't one of his buddies...

She refused to complete the thought. St. Charles was just an emissary. Part of a scheme to prove to her that the new Sheridan Weaver hadn't exorcised all of the old Sheridan Weaver.

She would not be fooled.

She pried her mail out of its long, too-slender box and frowned at the mix of bills and catalogs. "Junk, junk, junk." She sighed. Even the catalogs were uninteresting. At least Richard St. Charles had livened up her day. But that was no way to think. She didn't need lively days like that anymore!

With her leather briefcase and mail in hand, she started up the stairs to her overpriced third-floor apartment. It was a floor-through, with a bedroom overlooking an alley, a bathroom with a tub on legs, a kitchen that was just barely eat-in and a living room with windows that got full sun from the sunny side of Marlborough. Because the building had once been a posh town house, there were wide, curving mahogany stairs. Instead of opening at the top of the stairs, her apartment opened at the bottom, giving it a certain cachet. Also, she got to vacuum the stairs, not the landlord. It was the small rooftop deck, where she could grow tomatoes and geraniums, that had sold her on the place.

Sheridan fished her keys out of her shoulder bag and started to unlock the door.

And sensed a presence behind her. Someone, something. She couldn't be sure. She had heard nothing, seen nothing. But she knew something was there.

The years of mental and physical training went to work instantly, instinctively. She dropped everything in her hands and swiftly sent the hulking individual crashing to the floor with a simple hip throw.

As his body whirled through the air, she recognized the linen jacket.

He let loose a flow of curses as he landed and flipped onto his back.

Sheridan tucked in her blouse. "Sorry."

"That's a hell of a way to greet a guest," Richard St. Charles grumbled.

"Guests buzz on the intercom. They don't sneak up on people."

He rolled into a sitting position. "Don't pretend to be apologetic, Ms Weaver. You look positively smug. Proud of yourself, aren't you?"

She tried to look less exhilarated and more professional. "No, I'm not. I merely responded to a questionable situation."

"Well, I suppose if you did more of this sort of thing you wouldn't have an ulcer."

He swore more and got up, brushing off his pants. There was a rather large smudge of dirt on his left thigh. Sheridan tried to notice the dirt rather than the bulge of muscle. His body had the toughness of a man in peak condition, and she was grateful for her years of discipline and training in the martial arts. And also for her father. She had reacted more like J.B. Weaver than a black belt in judo. One of J. B.'s chief principles of operation was "deck the guy before he decks you and ask questions later."

"I suppose your father taught you that little maneuver?" St. Charles asked, none too pleased.

She shrugged. "I know a little judo and karate. You could have been seriously hurt, you know." She had been prepared to respond to any offensive move with a devastating snap kick.

"So I gather. But you restrained yourself?"

"When I saw your jacket, yes."

She wasn't sure he believed her. "And I should thank you?"

"No, that's all right."

He grinned and reached out a long arm. "I'm afraid you popped a button." He touched one finger to her stomach, and his voice took on an unexpected seductiveness, devastating in its own way. "There."

She glanced down and said softly, "So I did."

Her response was casual, but only on the surface. Inside a heady mix of sensations rushed out in response to that momentary physical contact. Strangely she felt energetic, alive, alert—more so than she had in months. Was it defending herself against a man like Richard St. Charles that thrilled her? Or just being near him?

Either way she had to get rid of him fast. She didn't want to be reminded of how much fun she had had working with J. B. and his entourage of friends and enemies.

"What were you doing, sneaking up on me like that?"

He had the audacity to laugh. "I was not sneaking up on you. I was right behind you and managed to catch the downstairs door before it latched. I just followed you up. I assumed you knew I was behind you and were just being coy, so I didn't say anything."

"If there's one thing I'm not, Mr. St. Charles, it's coy." She gathered her mail.

He snatched up her briefcase and handed it to her. "Obviously."

She sighed. "Still, I must be getting rusty. I should have heard you."

"It's the rubber-soled shoes."

"I guess. I suppose now there's no getting rid of you?"

"All I ask is ten minutes."

"Fine, then that's all you'll get." She unlocked her door and pulled it open. "After you, Mr. St. Charles."

She followed him up the stairs. He had good legs and an easy, altogether masculine way of carrying himself. Sheridan recalled the sensations prompted by his single brief touch. It was an unsettling feeling.

The stairs ended at a foyer of sorts where she kept her ten-speed bicycle and had tossed her beat-up running shoes. St. Charles looked at her over his shoulder. "Not as tidy at home as at work, I see."

She refrained from commenting and marched into the living room that she had decorated unexquisitely with pedestrian furniture and remnants of a more exciting past. On her rolltop desk without a rolltop was an eight-by-ten photo of her and J. B. in front of the San Francisco courthouse. St. Charles hunched over and had a look. "I think you have his chin," he said, then cocked his head around at her and grinned. "But that's all."

"Watch it, St. Charles, or you'll find yourself hanging from a lamppost on Marlborough Street."

"Impressive as your talents are, Ms Weaver, I don't believe you could get me down two flights of stairs—not without my putting up a fuss."

She headed toward the kitchen. "Who said anything about stairs?"

Once again came that audacious, charmed laugh.

"Do I amuse you, St. Charles?"

"Intermittently."

She got out a pitcher of ice tea, and he began rummaging in the cupboard above the sink. Unexpectedly Sheridan imagined how nice her life might be if she shared it with a witty and self-assured man who wasn't threatened by her own skills and intelligence. She shuddered. Richard St. Charles was *not* that man!

"You won't find any glasses there," she told him, reminding herself she'd promised him only ten minutes of her time. Surely he couldn't change her entire life in just ten minutes. "Bottom left cupboard. Wait—what are you doing?"

He dragged out a bottle of vinegar and was looking at it. "Tarragon vinegar. Well, at last a hint of Yuppie-dom," he said.

"What on earth are you talking about?"

"Yuppies are notorious for having all the best ingredients for gourmet cooking they never seem to have time to do." He checked the cap. "Unopened, I see." He returned the bottle to the shelf and peered into the cupboard. "Aha. Here we have lemon thyme vinegar, red wine vinegar, white wine vinegar, garlic red wine vinegar—"

"Must you?"

He shrugged. "I was just debating whether I should invite myself to dinner or invite you to dinner."

"Neither." The refusal was more of an effort than she would have expected. All too easily she could see herself at a quiet restaurant with this amusing, intriguing man. "You've used up two of your ten minutes examining my vinegar."

"So I have." He pulled two glasses from the lower cupboard. It was a small, adequate kitchen loaded with up-to-date appliances: a food processor, coffee grinder, pasta machine, microwave, juice machine. "You're going to be an interesting woman to figure out, Ms Weaver." He poured himself a glass of ice tea and nodded to her. She nodded back, and he filled the other glass.

He brought both glasses over to the tiny butcher-block table and sat down. But he seemed so overwhelmingly close that Sheridan found herself springing up and leaning against the refrigerator. She wasn't usually so jumpy, but something about the man set her on edge. She wasn't reacting to him the way she usually did to one of J. B.'s buddies. And certainly not the way she would to one of J. B.'s enemies. He handed her her glass; his half smile told her he'd noticed her reaction. "Thinking about pitching me out the window?" he asked laconically.

"Just talk."

"As you wish. Tell me, when was the last time you spoke to your father?"

She sighed. "You're supposed to do the talking, Mr. St. Charles, not the questioning."

"I begin to see why you have so many kinds of vinegar. Fits your personality. I am merely trying to figure out how much you might already know."

"Absolutely nothing, okay? I haven't talked to J. B. in more than a month."

"And saw him when?"

"At Christmas. I showed him the sights, and he told me he thought my job stunk, but my apartment was okay."

His black brows drew together in an intimidating frown, yet he said without emphasis, "Damn."

"That's it? Just damn?"

He took two swallows of ice tea and set his glass down. "Yes, that's it. You've told me all I need to know, Sheridan Weaver. Goodbye."

"Goodbye?" She couldn't believe what he was saying.

"Yes, goodbye. Obviously you know nothing and cannot possibly be of any help to me. Lovely and intriguing as you may be, I have wasted my time in coming to Boston." He rose, his tall dark figure dominating the small kitchen. "Thanks for the tea, Ms Weaver."

She gaped. "You're just going to walk out of here?"

"Unless you prefer to throw me, yes."

"But you're the one who wanted so badly to talk to me. So, dammit, talk!"

He walked back through the living room.

Sheridan banged her glass down. "Listen here, St. Charles, if this is all some asinine scheme you and my father have cooked up to lure me back to San Francisco, you're going to regret you ever set foot in Boston. Do you hear?" When he didn't answer, she raced into the living room. He was already trotting down the stairs. She leaned over the railing. "You tell J. B. I'm perfectly happy at United Commercial. Tell him I *like* being in a nine-to-five job. Remind him we had an agreement: he'd stay out of my life and I'd stay out of his. You got that, St. Charles?"

He stopped at the bottom of the stairs, his hand on the doorknob. "Ms Weaver, before I leave, let me clarify one point: I am not a friend of your father's nor a part of any scheme of his. I've only met him once."

"But—but how did you know I worked at U. C.?"

He looked surprised. "Why, I followed you, of course."

"Me? You followed *me*?"

"This morning, yes." He gave her the subtlest mocking smile. "Didn't you notice?"

He pushed open the door and disappeared.

2

SHERIDAN SKIPPED HER RUN and consumed a meager dinner. When she finished, it was 4:30 P.M. on the West Coast. She grabbed her phone and pressed the automatic dial button for J. B.'s San Francisco office. Lucille Stein, his part-time secretary for the past twenty-five years, picked up the phone on the second ring. She was a frugal, well-endowed woman, long divorced from a husband she never heard from, and she treated Sheridan just like one of her three daughters.

"Lucy, hi, it's Sheridan." She didn't bother with small talk. "I'm trying to reach J. B."

"Well, good luck. I haven't heard boo from him in almost a week."

Sheridan had expected, at worst, two days. J. B. was maniacal about checking with Lucille. "Do you know where he is?"

"Not this time, honey."

"You're sure?"

Lucille didn't grace that with a reply; she was always sure.

"Did you see him a week ago, or did he just call in?"

"Called."

"And he sounded okay?"

"Sounded fine. Is there something you aren't telling me, Sheridan?"

"A man's been out here asking about J. B. A Richard St. Charles. Tall, dark, good-looking."

"Oh, dear."

"Lucy, who is this guy?"

"I'm not at liberty to say. J. B. would pluck me bald-headed."

"Are you suggesting he's a client? This Richard St. Charles? He said he wasn't—"

"I'm not suggesting a thing. I got another call waiting. You want me to leave a message you called?"

"Might as well. Lucy—" Sheridan inhaled sharply. "Lucy, you'd tell me if something had…happened to J. B., wouldn't you?"

"'Course I would, sugar. Don't worry. J. B. can take care of himself. If he ever does me the courtesy of checking in, I'll have him call you."

"You're not worried about him?"

There was just the slightest hesitation. "No—and you know J. B. hates for anyone to be worrying about him. Now I gotta go."

Sheridan's apartment seemed eerily quiet after the call. She felt depressingly alone. She leaned back in her big comfortable white chair. Today just wasn't going as planned, damn Richard St. Charles's black eyes.

No, she wouldn't think about him. She needed a distraction. Her favorite P.I. show would be on in a few minutes.

P.I.s.

J. B.

Richard St. Charles.

Was he a client? But how? Clients didn't look for missing private investigators, and why wouldn't he admit it if he were a client? No, whoever St. Charles was and whatever he wanted with J. B., neither man had seen fit to tell Sheridan. Apparently her complacency was misplaced: this was no elaborate joke on her unless St. Charles was carrying his part to extremes. But she didn't think so. Somehow she had believed him when he had claimed to be acting strictly on his own.

That could mean her father was in over his head.

"Why are you thinking about this?" she asked herself. "You've got work to do. To hell with cop-and-robber shows."

Specifically, United Commercial work.

But instead of her briefcase, she reached for the Boston Yellow Pages. She simply had to get Richard St. Charles to tell her what was going on. If he had expected her to help him find her father and had planned on lurking behind every lamppost she passed, chances were he had booked a room in a nearby hotel. She flipped to the hotels and, starting at the top of the list, worked her way down, calling every hotel in Back Bay.

Fifteen minutes later, with a pencil tucked behind her ear and completely undaunted, she punched out the number of an expensive hotel in Copley Square.

"Richard St. Charles, please," she said. "I don't have a room number."

"Thank you, I'll put you right through."

Her heart pounded so hard she almost dropped the phone.

St. Charles answered on the second ring. "Yes?"

"St. Charles?" She breathed deeply so her voice wouldn't sound timid and squeaky; his sounded so deep and controlled. "This is Sheridan Weaver—please don't hang up. I think we should…talk. Please. I know you think I've told you everything I know, but perhaps I haven't. And, in any case, I think you haven't been very fair to me."

An ordinary man would have asked a few questions—would have at least hesitated—but Sheridan had already discovered Richard St. Charles was no ordinary man. "I suppose you're right," he said. "I'll meet you in the hotel bar in thirty minutes."

She didn't press her luck. "Thank you, I'll be there."

"And Sheridan?"

She loved the way her name rolled off his tongue. "Yes?"

"If you don't like what I have to tell you, just say so. You don't need to break up the place or attack anyone. I have a reputation to maintain."

She could almost see him smiling and was disturbed—disturbed because she liked what her mind was conjuring up and because she liked men with a dry sense of humor.

"I'm just a mild-mannered financial analyst, St. Charles."

"Yes. Well, see that you stay one."

HE HAD CHANGED into a black shirt and sat in a dark corner of the bar, a glass of an amber liquid over ice in front of him. As she moved toward him, Sheridan could see that his style—his manner of dressing, his quiet, uncluttered way of talking—was natural and unself-conscious. The man was just himself.

The dim light accentuated the blackness of his eyes and hair and the hardness of his expression. She would hate to see him truly angry. He was leaning back in his chair, stretched out as much as was possible without falling off, one arm thrown casually over the back of the chair and his right foot slung up onto his left knee. When he saw Sheridan, his one courtesy was to drop his foot to the floor. He did not smile.

She acknowledged him with a tight smile and slid onto the chair opposite him. "You don't look the least bit bruised or broken," she told him. It was a grand understatement. He looked nothing short of an uncompromising, beguiling male, and Sheridan was beginning to regret that she hadn't simply hopped on a plane and gone to find J. B. herself.

"We all have our ruses," he replied. Even against the background of live jazz, his languid voice was steady and quiet. He motioned to the waitress. "If, for example, I didn't know better, I'd mistake you for a remarkably dull businesswoman."

Wishing she hadn't gotten the conversation off to such a personal start, Sheridan ordered a glass of white wine from the cocktail waitress who appeared at her side. She had hoped her appearance would convince St.

Charles that the episode on the landing in her apartment building had been a fluke. Purposely she had put on conservative khaki twill pants and a periwinkle-blue cotton sweater. Her only concession to "cool" was to push up her sleeves to her elbows. She wore no jewelry and only a touch of plum lipstick.

"You don't know better," she told him. "You don't know me at all."

He shrugged and said, as if this explained her, "You're J.B. Weaver's daughter."

"So?"

"All day I've been trying to reconcile the image I had of J. B.'s daughter with the reality of the dark-haired lady in the gray suit. You had me confused for a while— even tempted to feel sorry for you. But no more."

For no reason she could understand, she bristled. "You have me figured out, is that it?"

"Let's put it this way: I know I don't have to feel sorry for you."

She would have liked to have heard what else he knew about her, but the conversation had already evolved into something far too personal for her taste. Besides, she was irked because she wasn't even remotely close to having him figured out. She didn't know a damned thing about Richard St. Charles except that he was everything she had learned to be wary of: roguishly good-looking, physical, intelligent, potentially dangerous. Despite her expertise at self-defense and her own crafty intelligence, Sheridan wouldn't want to bump heads in the night with Richard St. Charles.

"Is it hot in here?" he asked nonchalantly. "You look a bit pink."

She wasn't about to explain her inept metaphor. Her wine arrived and she took a sip, smiled innocently and changed the subject. "Thank you for agreeing to see me, St. Charles—"

"Richard, please."

That would never do. "I'm worried about my father," she proceeded. "As you no doubt have guessed by now, I haven't the slightest idea what you want with him. I don't know if you're a good guy or a bad guy or something in between, but I do know that I love my father and, for my own peace of mind, need to know that he's all right." She lowered her eyes, avoiding his warm, probing gaze. "I can't offer you anything in return for information."

"Yes, you can offer something in return," he said. "Plenty, in fact. But I'm not that kind of man, and you're not that kind of woman."

She looked up sharply and much too quickly—before Richard could do something about the heat in his eyes and the sensual intensity that exuded from his every muscle. If he had wanted to do something about those things. The bald fact that he wanted her was there, impossible to miss. She could feel herself responding, wanting him just as much, just as badly. He smiled, reading her look, and calmly sipped his drink, saying nothing. Nothing needed to be said.

Sheridan cleared her throat. "You're not a thug or a hit man, then, are you?"

He laughed. "No, hardly. Is that what you thought?"

"Fleetingly. You never know with J. B. Before I was convinced that you were a poker buddy of his and a fellow P.I. and that he'd gotten you to play along with him on some kind of scheme to get me back to San Francisco. My father tries to be understanding and supportive and all the things modern fathers of independent women are supposed to be, but he's not convinced I belong out here in Boston."

"Do you?"

"That's neither here nor there. This isn't one of J. B.'s harebrained schemes, is it?"

He shook his head, serious. "At least it doesn't concern you, although it could very well be harebrained. Your father and I met about a week ago on Vincent D'Amours's yacht."

The warmth she had begun to feel for Richard St. Charles vanished even more quickly than it had appeared. Vincent D'Amours. Her eyes narrowed. She appraised St. Charles across the small table. "You know Vinnie D'Amours?" she asked carefully.

"Not until a week ago, no. I was invited as a substitute in one of his poker games."

Sheridan nodded, but without understanding completely. Vincent D'Amours was a wealthy entrepreneur who often straddled the legal fence in his various import and export enterprises. He was also a compulsive gambler, a very good one, and the games on his yacht were legendary. Automatically, by virtue of D'Amours's reputation and her own keen mind, Sheridan suspected anyone who was invited to play poker with the likes of Vinnie.

"You said J. B. was there?"

"There were four of us...."

"You mean my father was playing poker with Vinnie D'Amours?"

St. Charles leveled a look at her. "That's precisely what I mean. That strikes you as unusual?"

Sheridan sagged, wishing she had held on to her self-control. She was getting rusty; a year ago she never would have given St. Charles a lead like that. "My father isn't in Vinnie's league."

"Financially, perhaps not, but he plays a hell of a poker game."

She said nothing.

"At the time, however, I assumed your father was in the same financial league as the rest of us."

The rest of us? Sheridan twitched uncomfortably in her chair. If Richard even approached D'Amours's financial bracket, his net worth had to be in the millions. *As the man says*, she thought, *we all have our ruses.* His millions might be as dubiously gotten as Vinnie's.

She sat motionless in her chair, watching him. *Who are you, Richard St. Charles?* She found herself very much wanting to know.

"To continue with my tale," Richard said, "toward the end of the evening, J. B. brought out a diamond necklace. He was short of cash and wanted to bet it. I was in a trusting mood—too much to drink, I suppose, and a natural inclination toward J. B. and a disinclination toward D'Amours, to whom he was losing and losing badly. If the necklace were real, it had to be worth around a quarter of a million. I offered to loan your father a hundred thousand dollars with the necklace as collateral."

"And he agreed?"

"Of course. It was all he needed."

Sheridan managed not to choke on her wine. "A hundred—ouch."

"Yes, ouch. He lost the hand to D'Amours, and I ended up with the necklace."

"Uh-oh. You couldn't possibly have believed—where would a private investigator get a necklace worth a quarter million?"

"If I had known he was a private investigator, naturally I would have wondered the same thing. But I didn't know. Neither your father nor D'Amours deigned to tell me."

"And the necklace turned out to be a fake," Sheridan surmised, shaking her head. How could her father have done such a thing?

"Yes. I had it appraised—not for a quarter million, but for five hundred dollars."

"Egad." She swallowed hard, the impact of what St. Charles had said sinking in. "Then my father stiffed you for a hundred thousand dollars, didn't he?"

Richard smiled nastily over the rim of his glass. "Give or take five hundred dollars. You catch on quickly."

"Oh, J. B., J. B."

"Obviously, when I looked up J. B. in the phone book and found out he was a private investigator, I realized I'd been taken. I decided to pay him a visit—"

"And Lucy gave you the line about his being in Boston visiting his daughter," Sheridan finished.

"Mmm, yes." He polished off the last of his drink. "I decided to find out what said daughter might know—as it turns out, nothing."

Sheridan nodded grimly, not certain she wouldn't have been wiser to have remained in a blissful state of ignorance. This was not the kind of news she wanted to hear from San Francisco.

"Has your father done this sort of thing before?" Richard asked.

"He's told people he wants to avoid that he's visiting me in Boston, yes. But passing off a bogus necklace in a high-stakes poker game—" She shook her head. "No, that's not like J. B. at all. He plays poker for fun, not profit. As far as I know, he hasn't played poker with D'Amours in years. Do you know if he was invited or just horned in on the game?"

"He seemed welcome. D'Amours has his share of bodyguards, Sheridan. I can't imagine anyone being permitted to stay against D'Amours's wishes. I gather he and J. B. didn't meet for the first time that night."

"Unfortunately, no, although I'd hardly call them friends. Before he made his fortune, D'Amours was a professional gambler. So was my father. My mother died when I was three, which was when J. B. quit gambling. He didn't think that was a proper career for a single parent with a young daughter, so he switched to investigating."

Richard smiled. "And he taught you all the ropes."

"Yes, of both his careers." She laughed herself, remembering. "J. B. taught me to play poker when I was four. It was just a game to me. Anyway, he's steered clear of Vinnie since. I understand Vinnie dropped gambling about the same time J. B. got his license. I guess he invested some of his winnings, but he was always better off than J. B., at least financially. I can't believe Vinnie actually let J. B. into one of his games."

"It's possible D'Amours was tired of playing amateurs such as me and was intrigued by the possibility of playing opposite J.B. Weaver again."

"But J. B. gave up gambling—except as entertainment, a reason for him and his buddies to get together Thursday nights."

"Maybe he's decided to go back to gambling now that you're grown up and off on your own."

"That's all I need."

"Sheridan, listen, I don't want all this to hurt you." His voice was surprisingly gentle, the roughness nearly gone, and Sheridan looked up, intrigued and a little nervous. He was stirring up her settled regulated existence. She wasn't sure she liked that. He smiled, the dim light glinting in his eyes. "Your colleagues don't know about J. B., do they?"

"No, I saw no reason to tell them."

"It's hard enough for anyone to get ahead in business these days, and if you're just starting out, this affair could hurt you. Look, I certainly don't need St. Charles the Sap added to my reputation, anyway. I'll do what I can to keep your father's misdeed from coming back to haunt you—and me."

She realized she was squeezing the stem of her wineglass so hard her knuckles had turned white. Slowly, so that Richard wouldn't notice, she pried her fingers open, put the glass on the table and placed both hands in her lap. Her heart was pounding. "Then you think my father conned you?"

"That's obvious, isn't it?"

"But you said D'Amours won the hand!"

"And you said he and J. B. go way back."

Sheridan groaned. "Not as friends!"

"As partners, cohorts, fellow gamblers—I don't care what. They know the game of poker, and they were there together that night. And I was the loser, Sheridan. I don't know the game as well as they do, but I don't mind taking risks. What's more, I can afford to." He smiled nastily. "The perfect mark."

"Which obviously annoys the hell out of you. But I happen to think you're being ridiculous—illogical, at best. You're seeing a conspiracy where there simply isn't one. J. B. wouldn't cross the street with Vinnie if he could help it, and I'm sure Vinnie feels the same. I don't know why he invited J. B. to play that night. But they didn't con you, St. Charles. How could they know you'd be dumb enough to put up the hundred thousand?"

He looked at her coldly. "I don't have to be nice."

"I haven't noticed you trying especially hard. Look,

you were the unfortunate victim of two pros. You lost, St. Charles. Go home and forget it. You have no one to blame but yourself for being suckered into putting up money for a fake necklace. I'm sorry you lost your money, okay?" She grabbed her bag, tore a few dollars out of her wallet, slapped them on the table and stood up. "If J. B.'s avoiding you, I can understand why. But I'm willing to bet he's just off on a case and doesn't want to be bothered. Thanks for the information, but you made a trip cross-country for nothing."

"I'll be the judge of that," he said in a cool measured voice that went straight to the base of her spine. "And I'll decide whether or not to pursue this business with J. B. But if he were my father, I would want to know where he is and why he bet a fake necklace in a poker game with Vincent D'Amours."

"He should be glad you're not his son."

"Sheridan—"

She whipped around. "Don't," she warned in a low voice. "No more. I'm finished. Don't follow me, don't talk to me. I wouldn't want to hurt you."

To her astonishment he settled back in his chair and grinned. Grinned! His eyes lit up, and he looked roguish and decent and amiable and disconcertingly sensual, all at the same time. She found herself wanting to sit back down, talk, laugh. She stared mutely while he gave her a mocking bow and said, "See you around, fair lady."

Disarmed, she stalked off.

By the time she had stormed back into her apartment, she knew she couldn't possibly leave J. B. to the vengeance and ire of Richard St. Charles without warning him. But to warn him she had to find him, and to find him she had to go to San Francisco.

She made a reservation for a flight first thing in the morning, packed enough clothes for a few days and had herself a proper drink, Scotch.

This time J. B. needed her help. St. Charles was cool, determined and capable, and even Jorgensen Beaumont Weaver at his best couldn't handle a man like that alone.

She put on her nightgown and finished her Scotch in bed. "And I can?" she asked herself.

Her mind flashed up a picture of him there in her cubby. Dark-haired, dark-eyed, laconic, quietly confident. Watching her. When she imagined the flat stomach beneath the black shirt, an ache spread through her, and she sighed heavily, swallowing the last of her drink. She was tired, that was all. Tired and worried and confused. But the ache remained, warming her, and she fell asleep dreaming of his tanned firm skin and his long easy stride.

In the morning Sheridan called United Commercial from the airport, said she was feeling under the weather and wouldn't be in and, as she hung up, felt a surge of pure exhilaration.

She could handle Richard St. Charles. She was sure of it. To be truthful, she was looking forward to it.

3

SHERIDAN ATE A LATE LUNCH with Lucille Stein in J. B.'s combination apartment-office two stories above Hyde Street in San Francisco. Lucy had picked up a couple of tuna fish sandwiches, and they sat in the small front room she used as an office, discussing events. Sheridan felt better just being around Lucy's ample figure, her stretch knit pants, her flowered polyester tops, her friendliness and her efficiency. Her hair had recently been touched up to its Marilyn Monroe shade of blond, and her eye makeup was as gaudy as ever. Lucy didn't believe in wearing lipstick to work, though, because it got on the envelopes when she licked them.

Within five minutes of bursting in, Sheridan had told her everything.

Now she was waving her pickle spear around. "Vinnie D'Amours, Richard St. Charles, a fake necklace—can you believe this? My father has finally gone nuts!"

"Now, now," Lucy consoled her.

"No, he has," Sheridan insisted. "Lucy, can you imagine owing a man like St. Charles a hundred thousand dollars? Well, can you?"

"Me, I don't owe a penny."

Sheridan could believe that. According to J. B., his secretary wasn't just frugal, she was cheap. It was a trait Sheridan had always admired in her.

"But you know what J. B. would say: if St. Charles was dumb enough to put up a hundred grand for a bogus necklace, it's his own tough luck."

"I don't think he's dumb," Sheridan said. "Impulsive maybe, but not dumb."

"Either that or rich enough that he can take that kind of gamble and not go hungry."

"Then why doesn't he just leave J. B. alone?"

"Would you?"

Sheridan sighed. "I don't like any of this. What in blazes has gotten into J. B.? I wish I could just *think*!"

She had had that long trip across the continent to think, but she hadn't been able to. She had filled the hours with second guesses and self-recriminations and, worst of all, disturbing thoughts about Richard St. Charles. Not about what he was going to do when he located her father or when he found out she'd gone to San Francisco, but about him and the altogether inappropriate attraction she felt for him. He was J. B.'s latest nemesis, and she knew nothing at all about him. Yet she kept trying to call up all the sensations that single brief touch of his finger on her stomach had aroused.

It was outrageous!

Finally she had decided her reaction to him was nothing but a throwback to the Neanderthals, primitive at best. Sheridan herself was not interested in primitive relationships—or primitive men. She wanted a relationship that involved, indeed welcomed, a meeting of minds as well as bodies. Sensitivity. Long talks, long walks. Shared ideals, shared goals. Sexual compatibility was important, but it wasn't the exclusive concern. She wanted more. Maybe she wanted too much.

Not that she thought she and St. Charles would be sexually compatible. Her daydreams hadn't advanced to that point!

But they had, and she knew it.

"How Neanderthal," she muttered.

Lucy chomped on a handful of potato chips. "What's that?"

"Oh, nothing."

She had to remember that: St. Charles *was* nothing. For the moment she couldn't permit herself to be distracted by absurd thoughts of romance, and nothing could be more absurd than the idea of having a lasting equal relationship with Richard St. Charles. Her single goal in coming to San Francisco was to find her father.

"I guess I'll have a look around, see if I can find any clues here," she said.

Lucy looked suspicious. She didn't like people prowling about her turf, J. B.'s daughter included. But these were unusual circumstances so she relented.

Sheridan took the second half of her sandwich and her pickle and started toward J. B.'s inner sanctum, but the ring of the telephone stopped her in midstride.

Lucy just stared at it.

"Aren't you going to answer it?" Sheridan asked impatiently.

"You know I never answer on the first ring." Lucy waved a hand. "Don't want to seem overeager."

"It could be J. B.!"

Finally, on the third ring, Lucy picked up the receiver and said calmly, "Weaver Investigations…. Where the hell are you? Yeah, she's here. Worried sick, too." Lucy handed the phone across her ultraneat desk. "You must have ESP."

"J. B.!"

"Hey, kid, how are you?" came the cheerful familiar voice from the other end.

"Never mind me. J. B., what's going on?"

"Long story and no time to tell it. Your license current?"

"Never the hell mind! If this is all some trick to get me back in the business…"

"Would that it were, Sher."

She stiffened, nodding solemnly. She had always been able to tell when J. B. was lying. And this time he wasn't. "How serious is this?"

"I don't know."

"Going to start at the beginning?"

"No time. Sher, I need you."

Her heartbeat quickened, and she hated herself for the rush of adrenaline, the feeling of excitement. "That's why I'm here, Pop."

"I want to hire you. Two hundred dollars a day plus expenses."

"No, I'm out of that racket. If you need a favor, it's done. But no money."

"I don't work that way, you know that, even with

you. Now look, all you have to do is keep an eye on St. Charles. I don't want him in my hair. Think you can do it?"

Sheridan gripped the phone, holding in her aggravation and remembering that her ulcer had started long before moving to Boston. "I'll need more information, J. B."

"What for? It's a simple, straightforward assignment."

"And if Richard St. Charles were a simple straightforward man and you hadn't stiffed him for a hundred thousand dollars, maybe I'd do it, no questions asked!"

"So he told you what happened, huh?"

"Of course. Wouldn't you?"

"Hell, no. I got more pride than to admit I'd been taken like that."

"J. B., did you con him?"

"Sher, Sher."

"I can't stand this…. Pop, where are you? Why don't we meet and—"

"Will you keep St. Charles out of my hair?"

"You don't know what he's like…."

"I guess maybe all this financial-analyst garbage has made you soft. I'll give someone else a call and—"

"Dammit, *of course* I'll help you. I just wish—"

"Terrific, kid, I knew I could count on you. Here, put Lucy back on, and I'll give her the okay to spring loose some cash."

"Pop—"

"Give me a week, Sher."

There was no arguing with him. Sheridan sighed, resigned to not getting any more information from this phone call. "Keep in touch, okay? I gather St. Charles isn't supposed to know I'm working for you?"

J. B. only laughed.

"Lordy Lord," she muttered. "How do I get myself into these messes?"

She handed the phone to Lucy and, clenching her fists at her sides, stalked over to the bay window and looked down on Hyde Street. She had just accepted an assignment as a private investigator. *Damn.* Her own ambivalence was undermined by questions, plans, possibilities. She was back in San Francisco, and she was thinking like a detective again.

Sheridan wasn't sure she liked that. But she wasn't sure she didn't like it, either.

Below her a cable car clattered by, and she was stunned to realize how much she had missed the city. The cable cars, the Golden Gate Bridge, the fog rolling in, the awesome vistas of city, mountains and ocean. While living here she had always seemed to be rushing about, working, never taking time to relax and enjoy the present. And she was still hurrying herself into the future. *Tomorrow I'll do this...meet the right man...get the right job...have enough money saved for a vacation.* If only she could enjoy today.

A shiny dark-green Porsche screeched into a parking space behind Sheridan's rented car. She saw the black hair, then the broad shoulders and tall powerful frame of Richard St. Charles. He was in gray and white today: pearl-gray pants and shirt, gleaming white loose-fitting jacket.

He slammed his car door shut and glared up at the bay window. Sheridan shifted to one side. Even from the second floor she could see the look of malevolence in his black eyes.

"Lucy, quick, it's St. Charles."

"J. B., St. Charles is here. You want to talk to him? No—wait!" Lucy banged the phone down. "Damn him."

"He didn't leave a number?"

"No. He knows I hate his seat-of-the-pants way of doing things."

"I guess so." Lucy had been grumbling about this for twenty-five years. Sheridan peeked out the window: no St. Charles. "He's probably on his way up."

"I don't hear footsteps."

"He wears rubber-soled shoes."

"You want to hide?"

"No, it wouldn't do any good. But don't tell him J. B. called. Just follow my lead, okay?"

The door opened and Richard sauntered in.

Sheridan beamed. "Why, hello, Richard. I was just having some lunch with Lucy. Would you care for some tuna fish?"

"No."

"A pickle?"

His eyes narrowed, taking in her and her sandwich and her pickle, and not with any indication of pleasure. "Sheridan, what are you doing in San Francisco?"

"I felt the urge for a visit."

He moved toward her, but she didn't take a step back, instead cockily popping the rest of her pickle into her mouth. "I said I'd forget this whole thing, Sheridan."

"Then forget it. Go home." She grabbed a paper napkin off Lucy's desk and wiped her fingers.

"What about you?"

"I'm none of your business."

Lucy gathered up the remains of their lunch. "Think I'll run up the street and get me an ice-cream cone."

Richard's deep voice stopped her. "Mrs. Stein, has there been any word from J. B.?"

Lucy hesitated, glancing furtively at Sheridan, seemingly oblivious to the deepening of Richard's frown. Over the years Lucy had become impossible to intimidate. "No," she said, "not yet."

"And you're not concerned?" Richard still addressed Lucy.

"Richard," Sheridan interrupted, "this is none of your affair."

She stopped herself, realizing that wasn't the thing to say. J. B. had lost a hundred thousand dollars of the man's money—not that Richard gave any indication of truly needing it. Money seemed to be the least of his concerns. Nevertheless, she didn't blame him for being upset. She glanced up and saw him arching a brow at her. He wasn't in a cheerful mood.

"Well, I suppose it is your affair—more or less. But I would prefer it if—" She stopped herself again. Here she was running off at the mouth with no thought to the consequences of what she was saying. "I have to think."

"A double-dip chocolate cone sounds good to me," Lucy said. "See you all…." She slunk out the door.

Richard sat in Lucy's chair and put his feet on her desk. Not wanting to look at the long legs and think Neanderthal thoughts, Sheridan paced.

"Would you care to think aloud?" he asked mildly.

"No."

"You know, here in San Francisco I can see you as a P.I. You don't look so self-conscious and ultra-Yuppie. I imagine your ulcer came after your move to Boston."

She scowled at Richard and told him to get his feet off Lucy's desk. It was a childish maneuver; he chose to ignore her. "You're remarkably annoying," she said.

"And you're remarkably beautiful. Do you ever wear your hair down?"

"In bed," she snapped.

"Something else to look forward to, then."

"What!" She whirled around.

He was laughing softly and sprang lightly to his feet. "Don't pretend to be shocked." He moved toward her, slowly, confidently. "You're not meek and you're not stupid. You knew what you were saying, and you knew what I would think."

"It was a slip of the tongue."

"Your back stiffens right up when you're doing your stodgy financial-analyst act."

He was toe-to-toe with her now, occupying her space, that invisible circle around her. She tried to tell herself she was occupying his space, too, but knew this wasn't true. He was doing the violating, not she. But—to her credit, she thought—she didn't move back. Her breathing quickened, and her body reacted in hundreds of tiny intangible ways to the nearness of him. But she stood her ground. She had work to do.

"My back stiffens," she said steadily, "when someone makes outrageous assumptions about me."

"Outrageous?" He smiled. "Tell me you don't want to kiss me."

"I don't want to kiss you."

"Now tell me you don't want me to kiss you."

"I don't want—this is ridiculous!"

His eyes gleamed with victory. "There, you see? That's not so easy, is it?" His hands—large, solid, warm—settled on her hips. "You're not ready to admit you're attracted to me and to take any responsibility for what we might do together."

"Richard, that's enough."

"Is that a threat?"

"I'd hate to bounce you off the walls. You've been so reasonable—until now."

"I'm still being reasonable." He laughed, the warmth of his breath reaching her mouth like a sweet gentle kiss. "An unreasonable man would have kissed you by now. Or perhaps not. Perhaps my restraint is a sign of irrationality."

Perhaps, she thought, hers was, too. She wanted nothing more than to hurl herself into his arms and go with the sparks crackling between them. But years of training, years of self-restraint, self-discipline, self-denial, held her back. A difficult-enough trail lay ahead of her without getting involved with Richard St. Charles. If she permitted herself a moment's indiscretion anything might happen, and anything couldn't happen. She had to finish this business between Richard and J. B. and get herself back to Boston. Back to work and the life of the competent, professional, dutiful Sheridan Weaver.

It would have been easier if Richard hadn't given her so much time to think, had just gone ahead and kissed her. She wouldn't stop him, though they both knew she could. He was right: she wasn't ready to admit her attraction to him.

"When we do kiss and make love," he said, "we'll do it together…with each other, not to each other."

The rough silk of his words loosened the muscles in her back. He stroked her sides with his fingers, then let go and moved back out of her invisible circle of space.

If her father were a fly on the wall right now, Sheridan wondered, would he change his mind about hiring her?

"Did you know I was here?" she asked softly.

"More or less." He sat on the edge of Lucy's desk. "I decided we had left things on a sour note last night, so I tried to call you at your office after I got back here this morning. When I heard you'd taken some personal time off, I figured you'd be heading to San Francisco. I flew back and drove on out here to J. B.'s office, figuring I'd have to wait. But you don't waste any time, do you?"

"Not where my father's concerned, no."

"I know you care very much for him, and I'm sorry I can't change the facts."

She narrowed her eyes at him. "You still believe J. B.'s a thief."

"I'm keeping my options open, but for the moment I'll give him the benefit of the doubt."

"For my sake?" she asked acidly.

"For mine, too." He grinned. "If I don't, I have a feeling you're going to pitch me out on my ear."

She couldn't hold back a laugh. "Ah, St. Charles, do I frighten you?"

"Frighten isn't the word."

"Unnerve?"

"No."

"Intimidate?"

"No."

"Threaten?"

"No."

"Then what?"

He didn't even hesitate. "Excite."

"I guess I should have seen that one coming."

"I guess you should have." He stood up. "What next, Ms P.I. Weaver?"

She sauntered—as boldly and sexily as she could in her spit-polished penny loafers—and stood toe-to-toe with him, violating his space this time. Only he didn't seem to mind. Up close his black eyes looked to her as if they were flowing, and she could see tiny lines at their corners, hints of amusement and, deeper down, desire. She felt brash, daring, devil-may-care. Her old self.

And there wasn't a damned thing she could do about it.

"I think the next item on our agenda," she said with assurance, "is for us to have a look in J. B.'s office for some clue as to where he is and what he might be up to...and for you to tell me more about Richard St. Charles. I want to know why you were playing poker with J. B. and Vincent D'Amours a week ago. I want to know who else was in the game. I want to know what was said, how people reacted when J. B. dragged out that necklace. We have a lot to go over, St. Charles. My father's disappeared, and I want to know why and where he is and what, if anything, it all has to do with you."

Richard appraised her with an intelligence and openness she found unsettling. "No wonder J. B. wants you back," he said softly. "You must have been one hell of a partner."

She sighed. "I was."

And until he was back, she would be again.

4

WHILE THE REST of San Francisco worked at being impossibly chic, J. B. and his office remained an island of functional tackiness. The walls were painted a dingy tan, the trim a shade darker. There were no curtains on the windows and no view.

He'd picked up his big oak desk twenty years ago when a country school up north had gone regional and had organized a going-out-of-business sale. The desk was pushed up against one of the short, windowless walls. J. B. had an army-green swivel chair with arms, and two four-drawer gray file cabinets occupied the same wall as the desk. On the opposite wall, Sheridan's former desk—cheap teak veneer—sat alone with no chair, piled with newspapers, files, cigar boxes. There was a blue corduroy sofa bed under the windows. Across from it were an L-shaped kitchenette and the door to the small bedroom. The bathroom was off the bedroom.

The entire place smelled of stale cigars and of a man who had gotten used to living and working alone.

"He's good at what he does," Richard said.

Sheridan opened a cigar box filled with paper clips and rubber bands. "How can you tell?"

"He's not into appearances, looking slick, obviously doesn't spend a lot of time sitting around here waiting for clients to walk through the door."

"When I was a kid, we had a nice apartment over in Sunset, near a playground. He got rid of it when I moved into my own place. He's never been into space, gardens. He bought himself a top-of-the-line camper and goes fishing a lot. He's more successful than this place might indicate."

"I don't define a person's success by the objects he or she owns." Richard looked at her. "Do you?"

She shook her head. "In spite of my twelve kinds of vinegar and assorted kitchen appliances, no. To me, J. B.'s always been successful because he's lived his life on his own terms. Except for my mother dying young, I don't think he'd change a thing about his life."

Richard said nothing, and she appreciated his silence, his tactfulness…and felt guilty for not telling him about J. B.'s phone call. But she was on a case now, wasn't she? Her circumspection was justified. J. B. had made himself quite clear: he didn't want Richard St. Charles anywhere near him. Never mind that Richard was willing to give J. B. the benefit of the doubt; J. B. wasn't willing to reciprocate.

Which meant Sheridan had to lie.

I'm not lying, she told herself. *I'm merely editing the truth.*

"We might as well begin with his desk," she said. "You take the drawers on that side, I'll start on this side."

Richard looked at her. "Sheridan, do you trust me?"

Sheridan pulled open a drawer filled with yellowed memo pads she had bought J. B. for Christmas one year

in an effort to encourage him to be more businesslike—
or more corporatelike. He didn't use them, but he didn't
throw them away. She didn't return Richard's look. "I
don't know."

"Do you believe me?"

"About the poker game and the necklace? Yes, I
think so."

"I want to find your father because I want an explanation. I think that's understandable."

Dully she nodded and looked under the pads, knowing she wouldn't find anything. "Yes, I agree."

"I'm not going to make him repay the hundred thousand if that violates the gambler's code of ethics."

"But you're not going to thank him, either."

Richard opened the left-hand drawer and winced at
the contents: a medley of used typewriter ribbons and
rubber bands. It was the sort of drawer things went
into, but never came out of. Sheridan had one in her
own desk at United Commercial. "Hardly," he said.
"What about you? Aren't you worried?"

Not as worried since I've talked to him, she thought
guiltily. "J. B. can take care of himself, but I do want to
know what he's got himself into. You said he brought
the necklace to the game?"

"Yes, it was in a black velvet case." He started on the
next drawer, which contained two staplers, boxes of
staples and, not least important, a staple remover. He
moved on. "It still is, as a matter of fact."

"What was he betting before he brought out the
necklace?"

"Chips, like the rest of us. He didn't start with much—five thousand or so—and he played conservatively."

Sheridan shut her drawer with a bit too much force. "Five thousand is a lot for J. B., Richard. Damn, I don't know what got into him! Did you get any indication that D'Amours actually invited J. B. into the game?"

"How else would he get in?"

"Maybe he invited himself, I don't know." She huffed. "There's a whole hell of a lot I don't know, isn't there?"

"I'm well aware of that feeling," he said dryly.

"What did D'Amours say when J. B. brought out the necklace?"

"Nothing. They were in the middle of a hand. I'd already dropped out, and Vincent D'Amours is a man of few words when he's playing poker."

Sheridan nodded. "Don't I know it."

"Do you?"

"Oh, yeah. I guess I haven't told you. I played poker with him once, a few years back. I was subbing for someone, a wealthy male friend—you know D'Amours hates playing cards with women, don't you? Anyway, this guy was annoyed with Vinnie and knew I was handy with a deck of cards, so he had me sub for him at the last minute. I thought Vinnie would choke. But he let me in the game, and since I was playing with someone else's money, I had a grand time for myself."

"Did you win?"

"Well, yes, but it wasn't that simple."

Richard was on his third drawer, though he wasn't

paying much attention to the task. His eyes were riveted on Sheridan. "Why not?"

She shrugged, wondering how she'd gotten into telling this tale. "Look, it's ancient history, has nothing to do with any of this, certainly nothing to do with who I am today and—"

"How much did you win, Sheridan?"

"Oh, it's not how much. A few thousand, anyway. It's just that...well, if you must know, one of the players was cheating, and I couldn't let that pass, so I said something, which gave Vinnie an excuse to turn his bouncers loose on me and toss me out. Of course, that was a mistake. I shook them off, collected my winnings and left."

About halfway through her admission, Richard had started to laugh.

"It was *not* funny!"

"You must have been one smug lady after that."

"Just for that," she said, "*you* get to go through his files."

Richard banged the bottom drawer of the desk shut and stood up. "There's nothing here, Sheridan. You know there isn't. This is a waste of time."

She plopped down on J. B.'s chair and put her feet up on his desk. Her penny loafers were getting scuffed. "In detecting," she said loftily, "one always has to go through the motions. A sometimes dull and fruitless task."

He glared down at her. "You're going through the motions to buy time. For what, I wonder."

An astute individual, Sheridan thought. He was looking down at her, studying her with half-closed eyes, and she could feel no irritation, no urge to run. She was tired, disheveled, a little dazed from the long flight, and she needed a bath, clean clothes, exercise. *Surely*, she thought, *Richard sees nothing in me at the moment. Surely he's only interested in J. B. and his hundred thousand dollars.*

"Buying time?" she scoffed. "For what? I don't have time to waste, Richard. You're getting entirely too suspicious."

"The Weaver family seems to have that effect on people."

He sat on the edge of the desk, his lean hip settling not two inches from her scuffed toes. She imagined taking her penny loafers and cotton socks off and running her bare toes along his hip.

"Egad," she mumbled.

"Hmm?"

"Nothing. If I'm buying time, Richard, it's to decide what to do about you." That, she thought, was a reasonable facsimile of the truth.

"You have no control over me."

She ignored the rough-edged quiet of his voice and removed her feet from the desk. "Nor you over me."

"It would seem logical, however, to pool our resources and work together."

"No, it wouldn't. It would seem logical for you to go back to doing whatever it is you do and letting me or J. B. get in touch with you when we've got this mess straightened out. There's no point in your wasting any more time on this. You can trust me. When I find J. B., I'll let you know."

"No."

Sheridan sighed. So much for that option. If he had been willing to resume his normal routine—assuming he had one—presumably he couldn't have gone traipsing after J. B and gotten himself and her into trouble. She could then have transferred her energy to the problem of locating her father herself. She would take one more shot at convincing St. Charles.

"Listen to me. Obviously—" She picked up one of J. B.'s stubby pencils. He never kept them sharpened. She remembered coming in every morning and compulsively sharpening every pencil in sight. No wonder he missed her. She began again. "Obviously I can't go back to Boston right away. The fact remains that J. B. isn't acting like J. B., and I have to find out why. Which doesn't mean *you* do."

"What you do is your decision," Richard said. "But if you stay, I'm not going to fade into the background."

"Not that you could if you tried." She grinned up at him, hiding her instant mortification at her impulsive words. "Forget I said that. So what do we do now?"

"I've been honest with you and told you everything I know about this situation. I suggest you do the same with me."

"What do you think I know that you don't know?"

"You tell me."

"A suspicious mind, to be sure. You know, you could hire me to find J. B."

"Hire you to—" He sprang to his feet. "The hell I will! You can find J. B. on your own damned time."

"With you as an adversary, a pest or a comrade?"

He stared at her. "You're on J. B.'s side."

"Of course. He's my father."

"I was hoping there wouldn't have to be sides." His tone was quietly accusing, not hurt.

"Maybe there won't have to be." She chewed on her thumbnail. "I wonder what would have happened if you hadn't been so idiotic and naive as to have lent J. B. the hundred thousand."

Richard didn't raise his voice, but it was deadly just the same. "I am neither idiotic nor naive."

She arched a brow at him. "Then how come J. B. has your hundred thousand dollars and you have his fake necklace?"

"A damned good question."

"Did J. B. look relieved when you offered to put up the hundred thousand?"

"To be perfectly honest, I don't know. He and D'Amours are hard to read during a game. I would have thought yes, but who knows? If he'd won the hand, none of us would have been the wiser."

"But he lost." Sheridan nodded, thinking. "I wonder if that was a surprise…or if he wanted to lose."

Richard made no comment.

"Maybe he wanted to stiff Vinnie, not you. If Vinnie had let him bet the necklace and won the hand, he'd be the one annoyed with J. B., not you. What about Vinnie? Had he shown any interest in the necklace?"

"None, and I offered the loan before he said whether or not he would accept the necklace as a bet."

Sheridan shook her head and shuddered, trying to fathom what it had been like for J. B. to lose a hundred thousand dollars of someone else's money. And all for a bogus necklace. "I wish I knew what he's gotten himself into."

"Maybe this isn't as complicated as you're making it out to be. It's possible, Sheridan, that your father has decided to leave the investigative business and return to professional gambling. The stakes are high, so he found himself an excellent copy of a tempting necklace, got himself into a respectable game and took his chances. He figured D'Amours would accept the necklace as a bet and he, J. B., would win the hand."

"No. He wouldn't take that chance."

"Then Vinnie owed J. B. a favor, and when J. B. said he wanted to make a comeback as a gambler and needed some ready cash, Vinnie offered me up as the sacrificial lamb."

Sheridan considered the possibility. "No, J. B. wouldn't go to someone like Vinnie to pay off a favor, even if Vinnie owed him. Besides, how could they have known you would have put up the money?"

"They're pros, Sheridan," Richard said darkly. "They'd know. I acted impulsively, but perhaps not unpredictably. And who can say what would have happened if I hadn't put up the money when I did? Maybe they would have suggested something."

"It's hard to believe.... No, I don't believe it. J. B. isn't ready to give up investigating."

Richard shrugged. "Perhaps."

"I admit it was a blow when I left, but not that big a blow. Anyway, he would have told me. We have a lot of options, don't we?"

"I'm glad you said we," he murmured.

"Don't get your hopes up."

She rose and stood beside him, unafraid but strangely exhilarated. Richard had a strong, healthy ego; she didn't have to coddle it. "You know, it would be easier just to put you in the hospital for a few days. I could straighten this mess out and—"

"Don't try it." He snatched her by the elbows and held her close, daring her to act. "I'd have you arrested for assault and battery, and I'd sue you for everything you own."

She smiled cockily. "Think what you could do with my twelve kinds of vinegar."

"You don't know it, sweetheart, but you're playing with fire."

His mouth descended to hers, grazing her lips, tantalizing. It was a brief, breathtaking kiss, and even if she had wanted to, Sheridan couldn't have knocked him flat. She could barely remain standing herself. He was everything she found intoxicating in a man—steady, virile, intrepid, black-eyed and solid. And everything she feared. He was a part of the life she had left.

He straightened but held on to her elbows. Very methodically, very distractingly, he massaged the flesh of her inner arms with his thumbs. "Nothing's simple anymore, is it?"

"I'm not sure anything ever was. Have you ever tried mocha-chip ice cream?"

He laughed. "Let's go."

Ten minutes later they were exploring the nooks and crannies of Russian Hill, eating ice-cream cones. Sheridan felt good walking beside Richard St. Charles. He was tall, strong and agile, and he didn't start wheezing and complaining after climbing one hill. His dark hair glinted in the San Francisco sun. And he liked mocha-chip ice cream.

"I love Russian Hill," she said. "If I ever moved back to San Francisco, I'd live here."

"You would?"

"Mmm. I like the scale of it. You can find just about everything up here, it's close to everything. Charming, but not cutesy. I can see myself in a little pastel place on a side street with geraniums in window boxes and a sun deck out back."

"What would it take to get you to move back?"

She grinned up at him. "The vice presidency of Bank of America."

"From what I've seen of you, I would say that's not too farfetched."

"Are you kidding? With J. B. around? He's raked up dirt on half the businesspeople in town, so I can't imagine who'd hire me. Anyway, how could I ever get any work done and secure any kind of reputation with him pestering me to join him in his nefarious schemes? No, it's impossible. If I'm to advance in a business career, I'd better stay on the East Coast."

"A moment ago you were talking like a private investigator. Now you sound like a businesswoman." He paused, peering down at her. "Which are you?"

"Some days, both. Some days, neither. And some days I just don't know."

He smiled. "Like today?"

"Like today."

They started down the steps of the crooked part of Lombard Street, past the gardens and brick curves. Standing in the warm breeze with Richard alongside her, Sheridan could scarcely imagine her life in Boston. It was a life of routines, challenges and order, a life she enjoyed. But could she go back to it? She shook off the thought; she had to. She didn't belong in San Francisco. She couldn't stay. She'd made up her mind about that once before, and she wasn't going to change it.

Yet even as she had looked up and seen him standing in her cubby, she had sensed that Richard St. Charles's eruption into her life had changed everything. There was a pull between them that made choices not nonexistent, but complicated, difficult, possibly even frightening. She would have to be cautious.

"How 'bout you?" she said, more lightheartedly than she felt. "Where do you live?"

He glanced down at her; his ice-cream cone was long gone. "Russian Hill."

She laughed at her own gaffe. "Well, I guess I'd better watch what I say in the company of a local, lest I sound too plebeian. Do you have a house or an apartment?"

"A house."

"But of course. And does it have geraniums in the window boxes?"

"It doesn't have window boxes. But it could."

She bit into her cone. "A sun deck?"

"Yes, and an overgrown courtyard."

"Do you like living in the city?"

"When I'm here."

"Meaning?"

"Meaning I'm not here all the time."

"Where are you when you're not here?"

"Are you researching me?"

"Suspicious, suspicious."

He walked down two steps before resuming. "I want to know if you're planning to use what I tell you against me."

"Of course not—unless you're the one who conned J. B."

"Don't be ridiculous." As usual he didn't raise his voice, but he didn't have to. He could make his point with a gesture, a phrase. His movements and his words were economical and effective. "Obviously J. B. is your motive for asking these questions."

"You're determined to be difficult, aren't you?" They were walking side by side, almost at the bottom of the hill by now. Tourists were walking up, taking pictures and pointing.

"I'm determined to get at the truth, to make you see what's happening between us. Sheridan, J. B. is not your only reason for remaining in San Francisco. I am, too. We are. I know we've only known each other a matter of hours, but destiny's at work, don't you think?"

She tried to get ahead of him, but he stayed beside her, matching her stride for stride. "Aren't things complicated enough already?" she demanded.

He smiled, as if something in her voice, her words, her face, had told him what he wanted to know. He seemed satisfied. "Would you like to take notes?"

"I have a good memory."

"I'm thirty-five. I have one sister, five years older, who lives in Seattle. My parents are retired and live in Hawaii. I grew up in Southern California, San Diego and La Jolla and attended Stanford University. I have degrees, a bachelor's and a master's, in history."

"History?"

"American history."

"Will wonders never cease."

"What did you expect?"

"I don't know, but not history. Did you get rich before or after Stanford?"

He laughed. "Your P.I. roots are showing, Sher. I'm what you might call of independent means. I inherited a little here, invested a little there—the usual route. I no longer work when I have to, but when I want to. I have an office in town and a very loyal capable staff who look after my interests and their own."

"How much are you worth?"

"What possible bearing could that have on anything?"

"I'm interested."

"You're nosy."

They reached the bottom of Lombard, and Sheridan popped the last of her ice-cream cone into her mouth. Her hands were sticky. "Most private investigators are."

"But you're a financial analyst."

"Right. Keep reminding me, okay?"

He took her sticky hand. "I'm worth more than a million and less than a hundred million. It varies from day to day."

"Fair's fair. I'm worth more than a thousand and less than a million. It varies from paycheck to paycheck. Now. Where was I? Oh, yes. If you're not on Russian Hill, where are you?"

"Sheridan…"

She removed her hand from his and wiped her fingers with a balled-up napkin, trying not to notice how warm her hand had felt in his. "Humor me."

He sighed. "I own a yacht and several smaller boats I keep in Sausalito, a cottage in Hawaii—"

"In my book, a cottage is four rooms or less."

"A house, then," he amended curtly. "You know, you could sound a little more intimidated by my vast wealth."

"Why should I? You weren't intimidated by my black belt in judo and karate."

"Fool that I am," he muttered.

"Go on."

"That's about it, except for Northwood."

"Not Northwood as in the horse farm?"

"Yes, Northwood as in the horse farm. As you obviously know, we breed and train racing thoroughbreds—

my current passion." He grinned. "My most recent passion, I should say."

Sheridan looked away, trying to ignore his innuendo. They turned up Leavenworth, walking back toward J. B.'s office. What would it be like to be Richard St. Charles's current passion? "I'm being compared to a horse," she scoffed.

"I beg your pardon?"

"Nothing. Northwood owns Savannah Sylvan, doesn't it?"

"Mmm."

"I remember when he won the Kentucky Derby. Such a beautiful horse. From what I've heard he commands enormous stud fees."

"He's not the only one."

She looked up sharply.

Richard laughed softly, moving close to her, and reclaimed her hand. "Darlin', I was speaking of my horses, not myself. If you're worried, I don't charge."

She cleared her throat, stiffened her spine and turned formal. "I didn't mean to imply—forgive me. I must learn to control my primitive thoughts."

"Do I look offended?"

She sighed. "Our relationship isn't going to develop normally, is it?"

"That's because it's special."

"Richard…" She tucked a stray lock of hair behind her ear, but it didn't stay, and she gave up. "Is there anything else?"

"About me? I should hope so."

"Anything pertinent?"

"I'm not married and never have been, and I believe nothing I own is worth as much as the people I care about."

A man of wealth, good looks, taste and sensitivity. It was all too much. "That's nice," she said quickly, "but it won't help me find J. B."

Richard exploded, "Damn that man for interfering again!"

She broke away from him, her hands going to her hips. "Don't you damn my father! If it weren't for him, we'd never have met—not that that would have given me any great problem. Damn *you*, Richard St. Charles, for making me forget why I'm here!"

"Because of J. B."

"Obviously! The more I know about you, the more chance I'll have of finding J. B."

"That's not true and you know it."

She was shrieking like a lunatic, and he was standing calmly, jaw set, lips hardly moving. She felt like flipping him, but that would violate everything she was and everything she had learned. Her skills were exclusively for self-defense, never to be used offensively. "Levelheaded men are exasperating," she said. "Dammit, St. Charles, you think my father's a thief. Why should I care if you've been married nine times?"

"Have you?"

She balled her hands into fists and lunged up the sidewalk. "Have I what?"

"Been married nine times."

"No! Dammit, no, I haven't been married nine times. I haven't been married once. I've never even been engaged. By God, I've never met a man I'd have!"

"Or who'd have you?"

"I threaten a lot of men."

"Most *people* are threatened by someone who's as self-assured as you are."

"I always thought it was my brains and brawn that threatened them."

He gave a small devastating smile. "Could be."

She laughed. "But you're not threatened?"

"Not at all, darlin', not at all."

"Well, maybe you should be."

"That would make it easier for you, wouldn't it?" He sighed audibly. "I was right, you know. Romancing you with J. B. and his damned necklace between us is going to be impossible."

Sheridan shook her head emphatically. "Wrong. If there were no J. B. and no necklace, we'd still be an impossible pair. Forget it, St. Charles. I admit there's an elemental appeal about you, but other than that...no, it's outrageous."

"But inevitable. We'll finish up this business with J. B. and see what happens."

"*I'll* finish up this business with J. B. and be on my way back to Boston."

"In addition to being stubborn, you're also bossy." He resumed walking alongside her. "I suppose you have instructions for me?"

"I don't need your sarcasm, Richard. What I need is

for you to forget about romancing me." There, she'd said it, bald-faced lie that it was. What she needed was for Richard to put his arms around her. Or at least that was what she wanted. She continued valiantly, "This'll be easier on us both if you do."

"Tut, tut. You can mash me to a pulp, Sher, but you can't change the facts."

"I'm not trying to change the facts, I'm just trying to get you to quit distracting me."

"Then it's all right if I continue to want to make love to you, just so long as I don't mention it?"

"No!" She rubbed her forehead. Where had she gone wrong? All her options were being reduced to a jumbled mess. She didn't know what to do: keep an eye on Richard, find J. B. or go home. Everything seemed so impossible. "Don't think it, either. Richard, I just want to find my father."

He touched the stray lock of hair dangling over her ear, but didn't try to put it in place. His voice turned serious, quiet, with no overtones of banter or desire. "I know."

She glanced up, her gratitude shining in her eyes. "So you can be a gentleman, too."

"If pressed."

"I don't want to have to choose between finding J. B. and getting to know you. Please don't put me in that position."

"Fair enough."

Smiling, he brushed her cheek with his fingers, sending millions of tiny charges tripping through her body. She managed to ask, "So what are you going to do now?"

"Hire you, what else? Three hundred dollars a day plus expenses. Find J. B. for me. Get this over with."

"But…"

He fished a slim leather wallet from an inner pocket and handed her two crisp hundred-dollar bills. "Your retainer."

She willed herself to speak. "Richard, I can't possibly."

"Dinner and a good night's sleep will get rid of the jet lag. You'll be able to think more clearly in the morning. I'll see you at eleven, in J. B.'s office."

He kissed her lightly on the lips, right there on Leavenworth Street. Then he walked away, leaving her standing in the sunlight with two hundred dollars dangling from her fingertips. She was too stunned to move. Who on earth did Richard St. Charles think she was? He didn't even know her! She hadn't told him about J. B.'s phone call, about J. B.'s insistence on her looking out for the man he owed a hundred thousand dollars.

Obviously Richard had made a mistake. He shouldn't have hired her. He shouldn't have decided he wanted to make love with her. He shouldn't trust her.

"You're going to be disappointed," she said to the empty space on the sidewalk where he had stood.

LUCILLE STEIN WAS BACK at her desk when Sheridan stumbled in and told her how she'd just squeezed herself between a rock and a hard place. "I don't know what to do," she lamented.

"What d'you mean? You're getting five hundred dollars a day to find J. B. and keep an eye on this character with the gorgeous eyes. So do it."

"I'm not a witch!"

"You'll think of something."

"It's unethical."

"Sounds to me like they both deserve to be played off against each other." Lucille handed her two hundred dollars in twenties and tens. "J. B.'s retainer for you."

"Oh, Lord."

"Me, I'd go out and have a big fancy dinner on the two of them."

Sheridan sighed and went into J. B.'s office. She put the money on her old desk and pulled up J. B.'s swivel chair. She moved the cigar boxes and old newspapers onto the floor. She got a dishrag out of the kitchen and dusted off the desktop. She brought the phone over and pecked out a number she could still remember.

Miriam Knight, a top metropolitan reporter for the *Chronicle*, answered on the second ring. Sheridan said hi and asked for everything Miriam had on Richard St. Charles.

"What in God's name are you doing messing with him?" Miriam asked.

"Bad news?"

"Only for those of us married with kids, m'dear. The man's got to be the sexiest thing going in this lovely city. He's straight, handsome, rich and dangerous."

"Dangerous? What do you mean?"

"Lives dangerously. Not your ordinary playboy, for sure. He's got all the right trimmings—style, money, reckless interests. You know, solo cruises to Hawaii, skydiving, fast cars, horses."

"Horses aren't a reckless interest."

"That's because they're one of your interests, and God forbid Sheridan Weaver should admit to any recklessness these days. Anyway, obviously he could have his pick of sexy women."

Sheridan said nothing, not wanting to incriminate herself. Of course, she had called Miriam because she'd known she could get this kind of information. Happily married though she was, Miriam kept track of San Francisco's available men.

"However, that doesn't seem his style. He was last seen escorting an assistant district attorney about town. Seems to go for intelligence and wit. Refreshing, huh? Usually your interesting, attractive, talented males don't go for like-minded women. Is he on your list, or are you on his?"

"I don't think I'm a like-minded woman."

"Ha! Get out of those stodgy business suits of yours, and I can see you two painting the town. What's your interest?"

"Strictly professional."

"Well, in case you're wondering, which you will no doubt say you're not, the assistant DA has been seen recently with a corporate lawyer. Perhaps she wasn't reckless enough for our St. Charles, hmm? Of course, we both know someone who's been known to jump out of airplanes, disarm desperadoes with a well-placed kick…"

"Your imagination amazes me, Miriam."

"Reporters have no imagination. We just observe and deliver the facts. What else can I tell you?"

Sheridan asked about Richard's various assets and residences and learned that, if anything, he had downplayed his net worth. Miriam suggested it to be maybe ten cents under a hundred million.

"But apparently," she added, "he doesn't really give a hoot about money—although he has plenty. He inherited a bundle from a grandmother or something and has made clever use of it, mostly in investments. He bought a couple of small, floundering companies, cleaned them up and sold them at a profit. I don't think he has a controlling interest in anything right now. He's pretty much loaded and carefree. Disgusting, isn't it? Look, kiddo, if you've got anything for me—"

"I'll let you know."

"Good. You've been missed around town, you know."

"Thanks."

Sheridan called in a few more favors, and by the end of the afternoon, when she was bleary-eyed and starving, she had the addresses of Richard's assorted dwellings; the locations, makes and registrations of his assorted boats; and the makes and license-plate numbers of his assorted vehicles.

She figured she'd earned her day's pay from J. B.

Then she picked up the phone and made one last call, to Swifty Michaels, J. B.'s closest friend and long-time poker buddy. Swifty tried to pretend he didn't know a thing about J. B. being missing. "He's on a case, I thought."

"You know better. He sort of owes Richard St. Charles a hundred thousand dollars."

Swifty didn't even hesitate as, in Sheridan's opinion, he should have. "J. B. can take care of himself, Sheridan—not that he wouldn't like having you back in the business, you know. But you gotta leave him alone sometimes."

She twisted her mouth to one side, her suspicions growing. "Swifty, what do you know about the fake necklace?"

"Nothing. Not a thing."

"You're lying. Dammit, this is my father we're talking about!"

"Oh, sheesh, I got a steak cooking, and it's starting to smoke in here. Good talking to you, kid."

He hung up, and Sheridan decided she wouldn't charge Richard for today. But how was she going to find J. B. *and* keep an eye on Richard?

By getting Richard to actively help her find her father. He liked living dangerously, didn't he? Probably he would get in her way, but at least she'd know where he was. She leaned back in her chair, imagining the two of them traipsing around San Francisco.

Fifteen minutes later she was ringing the doorbell to his house on Russian Hill.

5

IT WAS A SHINGLED HOUSE set behind a garden on a cul-de-sac off Green Street, not ostentatious, but not quaint, either. Standing on the landing, Sheridan could smell the rhododendrons and the first blossoms of the tiny yellow tea roses in the front garden. The fog had rolled in, and the air was damp and chilly. She had left her car parked in front of J. B.'s office and walked over, feeling at home again in this city where she had spent most of her life, but which she had chosen to leave.

Squelching a sudden image of herself walking home from work and putting her key in this door, she rang the doorbell. *Thou shalt not covet thy client's house*, she thought and waited.

Richard didn't come.

She pulled out her three-by-five cards and checked her notes; yes, this was the correct address. She rang the doorbell again and waited.

He didn't come.

She decided maybe his doorbell didn't work and tried knocking.

He didn't come.

She sighed. She was hungry, she was tired, she was

frustrated and her ulcer was acting up. Her evening was not proceeding as planned. She had intended to talk Richard into going over to her favorite Chinese restaurant in Noe Valley. She would tell him about J. B.'s phone call; he would tell her exactly what had happened at the poker game a week ago. Richard St. Charles wasn't proving to be as predictable as most men. Not predictable at all, she amended.

Unexpectedly she felt a tug of loneliness. The fog will do that to you, she told herself, admitting at the same time that this wasn't the reason for her gloom. She still had friends in San Francisco. There were a dozen people she could call up and invite out for Chinese food on the spur of the moment.

But none would be Richard.

"If it's like this now after a day and a half," she mumbled to herself, "imagine what it's going to be like in a week when you have to go back to Boston."

He had upset her orderly existence, and she fervently hoped she had upset his. She pictured him climbing out of his Porsche, the sunlight dancing on his hair. No, a man like that didn't have an orderly existence.

"You shouldn't think about these things when you're this tired, Sher. Go home, get some sleep."

She plucked a rose, stuck it in her hair and walked back out onto Green Street.

Abruptly she stopped, her heart pounding. What if she'd lost him? What if her trust had been misplaced and Richard *was* after her father? *Oh, God, have I blown it?* J. B. had asked her to keep Richard out of his hair. To keep an eye on him. And she didn't have the faintest idea where he was.

"Damn," she said, thoroughly disgusted with herself. Preoccupied with her own strange loneliness, she hadn't considered that Richard could be chasing after J. B.

Or maybe not. Maybe, without actually saying so, J. B. had asked her to keep track of Richard, not because he, J. B., was worried about Richard's getting *him* into trouble, but because he was worried about Richard's getting *himself* into trouble. The man, she had to admit, did have that air of devilry about him. But whether J. B. thought Richard was a pest or a candidate for protection, Sheridan hadn't done her job.

She raced back to J. B.'s, got in her car and drove over the Golden Gate Bridge to Sausalito, a picturesque town across the bay. The hills and skyline of San Francisco glowed in the early evening light, and it was almost as if she could reach across the icy blue water and touch the places she knew. The yacht club was easy to find. It consisted of a low cluster of buildings and an idyllic stretch of coastline, where numerous ships and boats of every size and shape bobbed in the water. Sheridan screeched into an illegal parking place next to the main building and was angrily waved at by the parking attendant. She jumped out, tossing him the keys. "I've got to find my father," she said, not having to try hard to sound winded and panicked. "He forgot his heart medicine—it's urgent."

She lied her way onto the terrace, too, where she found Richard, his back to her, looking out across the water at the lights coming on along the San Francisco skyline. He had a nearly empty drink in his right hand. Sheridan stood back, surprised at the physical jolt seeing him gave her. She wasn't only relieved, but thoroughly captivated. Even here he stood out. He was different, not because he tried to be, but because he insisted on being himself and only himself. He mimicked no one. His style, his build, his sense of purpose, were all uniquely his.

Or maybe her feeling for him made him seem that much more special. From twenty feet, without talking to him or looking at his face, she reacted to him palpably, uncontrollably, dangerously. In a sea of clones she was sure she could pick out the real Richard St. Charles.

She remained in the doorway, not moving toward him. He was safe. He wasn't out on a wild-goose chase after her father, getting himself and J. B. into deeper trouble, but here, having a quiet drink alone. And, she had to admit, he didn't look as though he needed her as a guard dog. She considered waltzing over to him and suggesting they have dinner together. But the club was elegant and formal, not at all like the Chinese restaurant she had had in mind. With her wrinkled clothes, scuffed penny loafers and hair sticking out everywhere, she felt like Cinderella before the ball.

And she thought, *I'm not Cinderella to his Prince Charming, and I don't want him to start thinking I am.*

Outside she told the parking attendant she'd accomplished her mission, then drove away.

Back in town she picked up some take-out Chinese

food for dinner, as well as some croissants and orange juice for breakfast, and made herself at home in J. B.'s office. Unable to bring herself to sleep in her father's empty room, she slept on the lumpy sofa bed. For a long time she stared wide-eyed at the ceiling, thinking of J. B...and, for a longer time, of Richard.

In the morning she called United Commercial and told them there'd been a family emergency, and she would be out of the office at least until the end of the week. She gave them J. B.'s number. By nine o'clock she was showered, fed and feeling businesslike and professional again. She shared her croissants with Lucille and updated her on her dual investigations.

"As far as I can see," Lucille pronounced, "they both deserve to fry in their own fat."

Sheridan agreed. "I just wish I'd gone ahead and told Richard about J. B.'s call. He's bound to take it personally."

"Of course he will. A man like that, a woman like you—things're bound to get personal."

Certain she had her infatuation with Richard under control, Sheridan drove out across the Golden Gate Bridge to talk to him at his yacht, where, she assumed, he'd spent the night. But he hadn't, and she had to turn around and drive back to the city. He wasn't at his house on Russian Hill, either. "There are just too many places that man can be," she muttered and went back to J. B.'s office. She had refused to panic. At six-foot-three and at least two hundred pounds, Richard St. Charles had to be capable of getting himself out of most of the scrapes he could get himself into.

His Porsche occupied her parking space in front of J. B.'s office. She had to go around the block twice before she could find another one and then had to walk. Yet there was a spring to her step she couldn't fail to notice.

"Uh," Lucy said when Sheridan burst into the office, "your eleven o'clock appointment is here."

Sheridan winced. "Oops, I forgot."

He was pacing in front of J. B.'s desk, but stopped abruptly when Sheridan entered. "Where the hell have you been?" he demanded, not raising his voice.

She shrugged. "Out riding around. It's a lovely morning, haven't you noticed?"

Today he wore a mulberry shirt and cream pants, no jacket. Although it had started out cool, it was supposed to climb to eighty degrees by midafternoon. Sheridan had started the day in some semblance of her old P.I. attire: jeans, jade-green cotton sweater and sneakers. Richard didn't seem to notice. He looked ferocious.

"I told you I'd be here at eleven," he said.

"I thought you were just kidding."

"I rarely kid."

"Of course not. I should have known."

"A parking attendant said you were out at the club last night."

Sheridan couldn't hide her surprise. Who was keeping track of whom? "How did you know?"

"Someone said I'd been watched by a disheveled woman in loafers. It could only have been you. I described you to the parking attendant, and he told me of your latest ruse."

Sheridan said nothing as she sat in J. B.'s chair. Richard didn't move, and she looked away, to no avail. She could still feel his presence, as if he were touching her. In her mind she could picture the tanned hard skin, the arrogant turn of his mouth, the black eyes, the wild hair. She shot him a look; yes, the reality measured up to, even excelled, the image.

"Why didn't you come over? We could have had dinner."

"You looked lost in thought. I didn't want to disturb you."

"You wouldn't have. I was thinking about you. Why were you there, Sheridan?"

Gotcha, she thought miserably, slouching. "I wanted to know where you were."

"Why?"

"To make sure you were all right."

"Why?"

He sensed something; she knew it. But what? How much? She looked up at him, realizing that none of her emotions were under control and that however capable and professional she was, she couldn't help wanting to know this man better. To, at the very least, be honest with him. "J. B. asked me to keep tabs on you. He knows you're not exactly thrilled with him, but he doesn't want to have to deal with explanations right now."

He didn't explode, which didn't make Sheridan feel any better. She would have been more comfortable if he'd gone for her throat, but he didn't move. There was no passionate feeling in the black depths of his eyes.

"Then J. B.'s been in touch with you." It was clearly not a question.

"He called yesterday afternoon, just before you got to the office."

Richard was tight-lipped and unamused. "How did he know you were in town?"

"I haven't the faintest idea, but I assume he was lurking around, saw me, found a pay phone and called. Richard, I know what you must be thinking, and you're wrong. J. B. called that one time, and that's it. We haven't been in touch on any kind of regular basis. I don't know where he is. I'm just as confused and angry about all this as you are—well, almost. I didn't tell you he called because…" There was no way of getting around the truth. "Because he asked me not to. He didn't think it wise."

His eyes bored through her. "He was right."

She leaned back in the swivel chair. Her sleeves were pushed up to her elbows, her hair dangling. She remembered, almost as if the scene had taken place in another century, that Richard had said he would like to see her hair down. Was that why she hadn't bothered with her various bands, twists and combs this morning? Not that this mattered. She could have dyed her hair pink and gotten a Mohawk cut, and she doubted Richard would have noticed. The interest of yesterday and the day before was gone. She felt not one tiny spark flying from his direction. What had happened to the talk of romance and lovemaking?

J.B. Weaver had happened, that was what. J. B., deceit,

filial duty and a fake necklace. Obviously Richard had the willpower—or the indifference—to put aside the longings he had proclaimed yesterday. Sheridan didn't. Now that he was here, close, she was anything but indifferent. While Richard was angry and uninterested, she was melting before his eyes. What had possessed her to insist he leave her alone while J.B. Weaver was on the loose? She wasn't sure she liked honorable men.

"You're not being fair," she told him.

"That, my dear, is like the pot calling the kettle black." There was nothing courtly about his tone; he was the same quietly furious individual who had tracked her down at United Commercial, suspicious and unforgiving.

Sheridan pushed her chair back. "You could be more understanding, you know."

"And you could be more honest." He turned, not making a sound, and snatched open the door. Sheridan was relieved to see that display of anger, however controlled. He glared over his shoulder at her, but she didn't flinch. "We're back to basics, dear heart. I'm no longer willing to give your father the benefit of the doubt. I want him, and I want a full explanation."

"Richard, for heaven's sake—"

He walked out.

She leaped up and banged the chair under the desk. "I could wrestle you to the floor and make you listen, you know!"

He kept walking.

"Don't get me mad, St. Charles!"

The outer door opened and closed. Hard.

Sheridan picked up a cigar box and threw it. "Men!"

Lucille was whistling innocently over her typewriter when Sheridan stomped through her office and opened the front window, nearly ripping it out of its tracks. Richard was putting the same effort into opening the door of his Porsche.

"If you leave, I'll just have to follow you!" she yelled.

Without so much as glancing up at her, he got into the car, started it and drove off. Sheridan let out a string of very J.B. Weaver-like language and grabbed her bag.

"Well, Sher, I see you've finally met your match," Lucille said, dabbing correction fluid.

"Lucille," Sheridan said, "go home."

THERE WAS NO WAY a rented compact was going to keep up with a Porsche. After losing Richard in the traffic at Fisherman's Wharf, Sheridan gave up, parked and decided she had to outwit him. Or at least try. The man had a temper after all. She didn't find that terrifying, but comforting, even exhilarating. He was human. She liked to be able to have out an argument with someone.

"If I were Richard St. Charles and I were in the foulest of foul moods, where would I go?" she asked herself.

I would want to be alone, she thought, *and far away from anyone who could worsen my mood—or perhaps even improve it. I would want to enjoy my bad temper to the fullest. I would...*

"His yacht."

This time she found a public parking place and

walked over to the yacht club, but arrived too late. Richard had already gone out, not in his yacht, but in his smaller boat. He would want to get away quickly, with lots of speed, she decided. *Damn him for being so…so…*

Sheridan sighed, breaking off the thought. How could she blame him for being angry? In his shoes she would have probably pitched him out the window for such a lie. Clearly the thing to do was to find J. B., convince him he needed her active support and get him to give *her* a full explanation. Depending on what J. B. had to say for himself, she would then tell, or not tell, Richard everything.

Where to begin… She was going to have to think and act like a private investigator.

As she started up the brick walkway back out to the street, a familiar voice hollered behind her, "Hey, kid, wait up!"

She whirled. "J. B.!"

He was lanky, gray-haired and rumpled, with his daughter's blue eyes, the same man she had loved and respected all her life. He flashed his cheerful smile and flung an arm around her shoulders. "Good to see you, kid. It's been too damned long. You're looking terrific."

"Thanks, so are you. J. B., what's going on around here? What are you doing? Richard—"

"Whoa, one thing at a time. I just lied my way onto St. Charles's yacht and had a look around."

Sheridan groaned. "What on earth for? J. B.—"

"The man's loaded, Sher."

"I know."

"He makes D'Amours look like a pauper."

"I checked into all that, J. B. Tell me something I don't know."

J. B. glanced sideways down at her. "So you lost him, huh?"

She wasn't sure she liked his probing look. "Be glad I did. If he were here with me, he'd probably wring your scrawny neck, and I wouldn't blame him!"

J. B. rubbed said neck—it wasn't scrawny—with the palm of his hand. For a man in his mid-fifties he was in remarkable condition. He wore baggy jeans, sneakers and a rumpled cotton shirt, and his hair would have defeated any comb he owned. Nevertheless, he radiated all the skill and confidence of the man who had raised a daughter and worked in a sometimes dangerous, sometimes dull profession. She hugged him, glad she was his daughter.

They sat on a bench overlooking the bay. J. B. busied himself retying his sneakers, not looking at his only child. "Sher, Swifty told me you're on my tail. Get off it, okay? I don't want you and St. Charles involved in the nitty-gritty of this business, okay? I know you've got a hundred and one questions you want to ask me. Just believe me, I don't have the answers."

"J. B., I can help."

"Not on this one. If I hadn't seen St. Charles with my own two eyes and didn't know what I'd be getting you into, I'd tell you to take him back to Boston with you. But forget that. The two of you together—nothing but fireworks."

Sheridan sighed. "What were you doing on his boat, Pop?"

"Looking for that damned necklace!"

"What! But why? It's barely worth five hundred dollars, as you well know. I can't believe you had the gall to bet it in the first place."

"All water over the dam, Sher. The man should be more careful with his money."

"Well, don't come crying to me when he catches up with you. J. B., where did you get the necklace? And what were you doing playing poker with D'Amours in the first place? You're not in his league. You don't even like him."

J. B. grinned. "Hey, you're sounding like my old Sher again."

"Out of necessity. J. B., you can't keep sneaking around. You—My God, if Richard had caught you on his yacht! You were going to steal the necklace?"

"Sure, it's not worth anything, like you said."

"Why?"

"'Cause it's a fake."

"J. B., be serious. I mean why do you want to steal it?"

"Listen, kid, this business is getting not only complicated, but dangerous. I don't know half of what I can guess, and I don't have proof for any of it, but I'm damned well going to get some. You're not helping me by letting St. Charles run loose. Will you *please* keep him the hell out of this? He could end up getting hurt, you know. Now I can't sit out here in the open and yak all day. Go find your St. Charles and—"

"He's not my St. Charles," she muttered.

"A slip of the tongue. Damned if I need a man like that in the family."

"Not to worry, J. B. You aren't going to ask me to steal the necklace?"

"Sher! Would I ask you to betray a trust? I'm wounded, wounded to the quick."

She scowled. "Give me a break, J. B."

"Look, just keep track of St. Charles for a few days, that's all."

Sheridan was spared answering by two men in tight-fitting knit shirts who rounded the corner of the yacht club. One man was very light, the other very dark. J. B. saw them, paled and leaped to his feet. "Fend 'em off, kid, I gotta get the hell out of here."

"Who are they? D'Amours's men? Richard's—"

J. B. was gone at a gallop.

The two men started after him. Sheridan debated letting them have him but, after all, he was her father. She jumped into their path, and naturally they tried to push her aside, which was a mistake. Employing both karate and judo moves, not to mention quick thinking, she hurled the light one into a bed of pansies and delivered a snap kick to the dark one. He crumpled at her feet.

From the water a deep, gravelly voice yelled, "Sheridan, what the hell are you doing? Damn it, he's got a gun!"

Expecting as much, she was already spinning around. The blonde was on his feet, fumbling for his gun. With a slicing kick she sent the gun skidding into the water.

The two thugs swore, gathered themselves up and retreated.

Richard was out of his skiff and bounding over to her.

"Damn," Sheridan breathed, "I haven't done that in ages. Wish I'd done some stretching this morning."

"Feel good?" he asked silkily.

She flipped her hair up, then let it drop, meeting his gaze. "Worked up a sweat, that's about it."

"Your eyes are gleaming, Sher."

His were half closed, no longer angry, studying her with a mysterious, captivating smile. "Exertion does that to me." She stood on her tiptoes, looking beyond him. "I should go after them."

"They're long gone by now."

So, she hoped, was her father. "I take it they're not yours?"

He smiled. "Still don't trust me, Sheridan? No, they're not mine. I fight my own battles, legally and without violence. I don't employ thugs."

She tilted her chin at him. "I believe you."

"Then we're making progress. They weren't random thugs, were they?"

"No, I don't think so." They were standing close. Richard smelled of hard physical work and the sea; perspiration glistened on his forehead. He was obstinate, but she didn't want to lie to him. "I'm pretty sure they were after J. B."

"J. B.," he repeated.

"Yes. He was here."

"I know, I saw him. I watched you two having your

little tête-à-tête, and I watched him run." His voice was low, deadly. "He's good at running, isn't he?"

"He knew I could handle the situation. They were after him, not me. And I didn't see you leaping to my rescue, Mr. St. Charles."

He surprised her by laughing, not a reserved chuckle, but a head-thrown-back, from-the-gut laugh. It set the hair on the back of her neck on end and started an ache swelling inside her, one that wasn't remotely connected to her ulcer. It was the sort of laugh that would haunt a woman's dreams forever.

"Sweetheart," he said, "I debated warning those two sods what they'd gotten themselves into. You're one lovely and dangerous woman, Sheridan Weaver…and looking less and less like a financial analyst every hour."

She pursed her lips. "Aren't you supposed to be mad at me?"

"I am mad at you." He spoke in his sandpapery voice, rough, but with the ability to smooth, finish, glide. "I'm furious, in fact. Let's go aboard my yacht, have lunch and talk."

"But J. B…"

"Long gone, Sher."

"I should make sure he got away, at least."

"I have a feeling J. B. *always* gets away."

She frowned, a lock of hair dropping forward. "Do you have an answer for everything?"

"No, not everything. For instance, I don't know why I can't stop thinking about you." The corners of his mouth turned upward in something resembling a smile, and his eyes softened. "I think the prospect of being alone with me on my boat makes you more nervous than decking those two goons did."

"That's not true," she said, not convincing even herself.

"Then let's go."

"Must you always be so matter-of-fact? Why don't you just argue with me! Say, 'Sheridan, it is true, damn it, and here's why.' Why do you always have to call my bluff? You're always so damned direct! 'Then let's go'— what's that supposed to mean? You can drive a person crazy, you know. It's a wonder D'Amours and J. B. didn't clean you out at that poker game! You have no finesse whatsoever. You—What are you shaking your head about?"

"How one moment you can be the ultracompetent, ultracool Sheridan Weaver and the next sound like a complete lunatic. Oh, but I apologize for my lack of finesse, of course." He was very close to her and finally lifted one finger, just grazing her chin; the ache inside her swelled almost beyond control. He gave her a dark smile. "I have finesse, darlin', where and when it counts."

She sprang two steps backward. "That's it, no way am I getting on any boat with you."

"Coward."

"I am not a coward! I've just weighed the pros and cons and going out to your yacht comes up short."

"Fine." There was no sign he was losing patience. "We'll sit here and talk."

"We won't, either. I'm starving."

"I have crabmeat salad and croissants aboard, wine, fresh raspberries."

"You're a stubborn man, Richard St. Charles...but how can I turn down fresh raspberries? Will you promise you won't pitch me overboard when I tell you about J. B.?"

A grin lit up his eyes, loosened the stiffness of his jaw. "I never try anything at which I have no prospect whatsoever of succeeding."

"Except playing poker with my father. Then you promise?"

"I promise not to even try to pitch you overboard."

They had a look around the club's lot and the street, saw no sign of J. B. or the thugs and headed out to the yacht. It wasn't until Sheridan was climbing out of the launch, Richard's hands lightly on her waist, that she realized a man like him would be a stickler about his words. He had promised not to throw her overboard.

That was all he had promised.

6

THEY SAT in stark white canvas chairs on the deck and looked out across the churning blue waters of the bay to the San Francisco skyline. Richard had brought up two tall glasses of ice tea. They drank in silence, neither knowing where to begin.

Finally Richard said quietly, evenly, "The next time I'm angry with you, I promise I won't stomp off. It's not my style. I apologize."

"I hope never to see you quite that angry again."

"Oh, you will. We're both too strong-minded and passionate not to get furious with each other once in a while. It will happen, and it should."

He seemed to be taking in not only today, but tomorrow as well, and next month, next year. Their entire lives. Sitting there in the sun, drinking tea with him, she could see it herself: a lifetime of arguments, adventures, lovemaking.

She kicked out her legs suddenly, locking her knees to help steel herself against the onslaught of inappropriate and hopeless feelings. Yes, it was possible that Richard St. Charles was the man for the former Sheridan Weaver, P.I. That Sheridan had always dreamed of a man who would be adventurous, spirited and honest and handsome and rich and gravel-voiced. Why not? In those days she had dared to dream anything.

Not anymore. Through long hours of study, through self-denial and self-discipline, she had put order and stability into her life. Never before had she had a reliable schedule, a reliable paycheck, a reliable way of life. In Boston, working at U. C., she did.

That ordered life had been blown to bits by the man slouched so languidly, so damned insolently, in the chair beside her. He was a threat to the woman she had become. This she would have to remember.

"Then you're sorry you got so mad about J. B.'s hiring me to keep an eye on you?" she asked.

"I didn't say that. I said I was sorry I'd stomped out on you during the heat of the moment."

She didn't know what to say. "I see."

"I don't like dishonesty."

"I wasn't dishonest!"

"Then what were you?"

She considered that for a moment. "Caught between a rock and a hard place. I still am."

"Are you afraid of telling me the truth, Sheridan? I can't believe you're so insecure as to resort to deceit. You don't have to be less than you are, Sheridan. That insults me. Being everything you are—" he smiled suddenly, sitting back, "—intrigues me."

"That's refreshing," she said, trying to suppress a purely physical reaction to him. "I scare the hell out of a lot of men."

"Only the weak ones."

"And you're not weak."

His smile grew reflective, even more enigmatic. "No, I don't think so. Sheridan, I don't think you tried to spare me or lie to me. Not really. I doubt that you've ever been less than straight with someone...unless you felt you had to be. Caring about others, like your father, is one thing. Tearing yourself apart to accomplish that isn't good. It's self-destructive and deceitful. And that's not the way I picture Sheridan Weaver. You're impulsive, occasionally reckless and cocky as hell, but you're not self-destructive."

He sipped his ice tea, holding his glass lightly between his fingertips, and looked at her. She said nothing, amazed. This was the most she had heard him say at one time, and none of it made sense. She wasn't self-destructive, to be sure, but neither was she impulsive or reckless. And cocky as hell? *Her?* Certainly not.

"Just last week the vice-president in charge of my department called me a capable, prudent and businesslike financial analyst."

"I'm sure you are, but that has nothing to do with you personally."

"How would you know? Obviously you don't know me very well at all, Richard."

He shook his head. "With us, Sheridan, minutes are whole hours, hours whole days. I understand you better than I've understood any woman, and I'm intrigued far more than I've ever been. I want to know you better, but I feel I know you well. Now talk to me, Sheridan."

She shifted awkwardly in the chair. It was a remarkably comfortable piece of furniture, but she was uncomfortable, made so by the truth of Richard's statement and his eerie insight. Perhaps he was right. Perhaps their intense hours together had shown him more about her than she had meant to reveal.

"J. B. hired you, didn't he?"

She tugged at her sweater. "I'm getting hot."

"Didn't he, Sheridan?"

"Yes, all right! He did, and I don't blame him. He wants you out of his hair—that's all." She took a big gulp of ice tea. "I feel like a grilled swordfish. Anything else?"

"How much is he paying you?"

The man was relentless. "You think I'd take money—" She sighed, unable to complete the lie; obviously Richard had already guessed the truth. "Two hundred a day plus expenses."

"His two hundred plus my three hundred adds up to five hundred a day."

"You're brilliant, Richard."

"You're making a killing on us, aren't you?"

"If you both weren't so damned pigheaded and *believed* me when I say I don't want to do any more investigative work, I wouldn't be in this situation!"

"It's always easier to blame others for decisions we freely make."

"I didn't make any decision freely! How many times have I said I just want to find J. B., help him get out of whatever trouble he's in and go back to Boston? I can't help it if you don't believe me!"

"Sheridan, you're turning red. What are you doing in a sweater on a day like today?"

She set her glass down on the little white table beside her, stretched out in the chair and stared up at the sky. "Maalox," she said, "I need Maalox."

"I suggest you go below and put on one of my shirts before you collapse of heat prostration."

She eyed him. "I'll live."

He looked at her mildly, his eyes gleaming. "Of course, I could drag you below myself and—"

"That I'd like to see!"

"There you go, cocky as hell. Sheridan, just because you caught me off guard once doesn't meant I can't haul your lovely behind down a few steps if I put my mind to it."

"Is that a threat, Mr. St. Charles?"

"I suggest you start moving."

Another of J.B. Weaver's axioms was don't push your luck. Sheridan got moving. She stepped over Richard's outstretched ankles, stopped and looked down at him. "You see? If I were reckless and impulsive, I'd call your bluff. However, I'm nothing if not prudent." She smiled, confident, maybe even cocky. "But don't follow me."

He smiled back, just as confident—and certainly cocky. "Is that a threat, Ms Weaver?"

Without answering him, she turned on her heel and went below. His stateroom was easy enough to find—it was luxurious and dominated by a bed the size of Utah. She found a soft mauve-colored cotton shirt in a drawer and put it on the bed while she peeled off her sweater. The cool air of the stateroom relieved her over-heated skin. She unhooked her front-clasp bra, exposing her breasts.

Just as at her apartment, she felt Richard's presence, but this time he didn't feel like an intruder, and when she turned, she wasn't ready to attack. He was leaning against the doorframe, watching her silently. She didn't scramble to reclasp her bra. His gaze fell from her eyes to her breasts, which were full and round, tingling from the coolness of the stateroom and the heat of his eyes. The nipples were pink and hard. She caught the two ends of the clasp.

"Don't," he said, but it wasn't a command. It was a request, a quiet, sensual plea.

She didn't, but refused to consider why. He moved toward her, gliding across the room, and his arms opened as he reached her. And she went to him.

First there was the feel of his body against hers, the warmth and hardness of his chest, the smooth, cool expanse of her stomach and back, the fullness of her soft breasts. Her muscles were well shaped, firm from years of exercise, and his hands reveled in touching her.

And then there was the feel of his mouth against hers and the sound of her own soft moan as her breath mingled with his. Her lips were already parted, precluding any chance to be falsely prim. Faced with her own fierce attraction, she couldn't exert what remained of her decimated willpower and rationality.

"You're just as beautiful as I had envisioned," he whispered into her mouth.

She molded herself to him, feeling the toughness of his long body, the desire he had for her. They could play mind games. They could argue and pretend. But their bodies cut right to the truth: she was a woman, he was a man, and they wanted each other more desperately than they had ever wanted anything or anyone.

His hands, warm and exciting, slid up her sides, angled between their bodies and cupped her breasts, teasing the buds of her nipples until she opened her mouth wider, responding to the primitive, erotic pulse of their kiss.

"We should have done this from the beginning," he said. "You wanted to. We both did."

"I didn't think you could tell. I thought you didn't care, not really."

"I do care."

He smiled, his hands brushing her breasts, then her sides, down to her hips. She could no longer feel the coolness of the stateroom. Her skin burned and her body ached. She was throbbing, swelling, with desire.

Richard's hands dropped to his sides. He said nothing; he didn't need to. He looked away, and she could see the way his jaw was clamped shut, steeling himself against himself. She knew how he felt. She turned quickly, clasping her bra and snatching up his shirt. She threw it on.

"It's okay," she said. "You can turn around."

He reached over and gently pulled her hair from inside the shirt, letting it tumble down her back. The shirt's shoulder seams drooped halfway to her elbows, and the hem came almost to her knees.

He stepped back, watching her. "Aren't you going to comment on my incredible self-restraint?"

"What self-restraint?" she said with a laugh. "If you had any self-restraint, Mr. Voyeur, you'd have stayed on deck!"

He grinned roguishly. "I wanted to see if you'd follow through on your threat."

"That's all?"

"No."

She grabbed her sweater and started past him, but he touched her elbow, stopping her. His eyes were black shadows, alive with bridled passion. Could he guess that his touch had set off new sparks inside her? The confident turn of his mouth, the angle of his jaw, the dark hair of his forearms, the sleekness of his body— everything about him seemed to demand a physical response. The kiss had titillated; it had not satisfied.

"Sheridan," he said, an urgency to that tough-tender voice, "I'll warn you now. I've exhausted whatever self-restraint I have. What I want to do, what I've wanted to do since I first saw you, is to grab you and make love to you until we're both too tired to do anything but sleep. Then we'll wake up and make love again. Do you understand, Sheridan? I don't give a damn about J.B. Weaver, and I don't give a damn about the necklace. I only give a damn about you, about us."

"I understand," she said, her lips suddenly parched.

BY LOOKING OUT across the bay and refusing even to glance at Richard, Sheridan slowly regained enough professionalism to broach the subject of her father. Picking at her crab meat, she said, "J. B. searched your yacht to find the fake necklace and steal it back." She paused, though Richard apparently had nothing to say. So she resumed, recapping her conversation with her father without editorializing. Richard could draw his own conclusions.

Which he did. "Then you're still working for him."

"Well…"

"Yes, well."

His cold arrogant tone finally prompted Sheridan to turn and look at him. He was on his feet, slouched against the railing, his eyes lost in shadow. It was all she could do to keep herself seated. A simpler alternative would have been to leap off the yacht and swim to Alaska. Her smile was more like a grimace. "I must irritate the hell out of you," she said.

"Sometimes." His face was expressionless. "But you always interest me more."

It was as if he were kissing her again. She could feel the heat of his mouth on hers and the hardness and excitement of his body molded to her. She had to look away quickly. "Of course I'll return your retainer and take myself off your case. I've seen J. B., talked to him and reported back to you. I've done all I'm going to do."

"Then you're going back to Boston?"

"No. I don't like any of this, Richard. I don't like it that my father was playing poker with Vincent D'Amours, I don't like it that he put up a fake necklace, I don't like it that he took your money. I don't like having unidentified thugs chasing him, and I don't like knowing he snuck onto your yacht in an effort to steal back a necklace that for all practical purposes is worthless."

"What do you propose to do?"

"Right now I'm not sure. J. B.'s no dummy, but I want answers. The key seems to be the necklace, doesn't it?"

"Yes. Did he ask you to steal it from me?"

She turned and looked at him. "For that I should toss you into the ocean."

Richard wasn't intimidated. "Did he, Sheridan?"

"He might have, but I told him I wouldn't do it."

"And I suppose I should applaud you?"

She put her plate on the table beside her. Why did she care what Richard St. Charles thought? Their kiss had been sexually exciting. Thrilling, in fact. A physical attraction, however, was not enough. He wanted her because she was different from what he was used to. That was all. "No," she replied coolly, "I'm not looking for accolades. You asked a question, and I answered it. I'm trying to be fair."

"Ah, I see. We have the MBA Sheridan Weaver at work here. Tell me, Ms Weaver, would you like to see the necklace? Would you like to know where it is?"

Her fingers itched and her stomach burned, not with desire, but with ulcers. "I wouldn't bait me if I were you, Richard."

"If you were me." He was quietly sarcastic.

Certainly looking at him now was perfectly safe, given her annoyance. She glanced up, but she was wrong. Looking at him was just as dangerous as it had

been from the beginning. This she found more disturbing than his sarcasm. She twisted her fingers together.
"I'll give J. B. twenty-four hours. If he doesn't get in
touch with me, I'm going after him."

He gave her an appraising look. "And what will you
do in the meantime?"

She rose and gave *him* an appraising look. Two could
play at his game. "Nothing."

Straightening from the railing, Richard surprised her
with a rich, sensual laugh. She could have screamed in
frustration. He should be predictable. He should be a
toad. Of all people, Richard St. Charles shouldn't be
caught up in one of her father's schemes.

"Then I'm on my own?" he asked, recovering his
easygoing demeanor.

"Yes."

"If I get into trouble, you won't be there to swoop to
my rescue?"

She looked at him levelly, trying to ignore the gentle
flutter in her stomach. He was too attractive. "That's
right. Therefore, I suggest you don't get into trouble.
J. B. is worried that you could place yourself in danger
if you continue to pursue this."

"Of course." He smiled thoughtfully, his mouth
twisting to one side. "And naturally this has nothing
whatsoever to do with what happened below?"

She looked at him levelly, but her hands were folded
tightly across her stomach, trying to quell the churning
there. More than her ulcer was acting up now. "Naturally," she managed.

"You're going to forget we ever kissed."

"I think that's best, yes."

"Good luck, darlin', because I don't think you can."

After taking her back to the club, he gave her a big grin and said, "Farewell, fair lady," and watched her stomp off.

On her way back to the city, she stopped at a drugstore and bought herself a bottle of Maalox.

AFTER SHE HAD TALKED herself out of going up to D'Amours's place and asking him if *he* knew what J. B. was up to, Sheridan sat in her car outside J. B.'s Hyde Street office and squeezed the steering wheel in frustration. She would give J. B. the twenty-four hours, but she wasn't the type just to sit around and do nothing. What could she do?

"Follow Richard around," she said aloud.

Any sensible private investigator who wasn't emotionally involved would retain a healthy skepticism toward anything Richard St. Charles did or said. He had been in the D'Amours poker game. He had lent a stranger a hundred thousand dollars for an unappraised necklace. He had flown all the way to Boston to find the stranger's daughter and, he had hoped, the stranger. He still had the fake necklace that, for whatever reasons, the stranger now wanted back.

Of course, the stranger was her father, and Richard St. Charles wasn't just another rich gambler. Like it or not, she *was* emotionally involved. And she couldn't separate her emotions from what she chose to do. She didn't want to.

Somewhere, sometime, she had to take the risk of trusting.

"Difficult, difficult," she muttered. "But I'll do it. J. B. gets twenty-four hours, and I leave Richard to his own devices."

Sheridan climbed out of the car and slammed the door because she hated herself for being so damned honorable. She hated waiting. She hated putting herself in the background. Twenty-four hours! She'd go nuts.

Yet she had analyzed the situation, and this was the appropriate thing to do.

She walked over to Union Street and went shopping, buying several less conservative skirts and dresses to add to the small wardrobe she had brought from Boston. J. B. might be back with an explanation tomorrow, but she didn't hold out much hope of that. And she didn't want her movements hindered by lack of clean clothes: her motto was always be prepared. The black silk dinner dress she tried on at an expensive boutique, however, had no functional use. She could just imagine herself wearing it to dinner at an elegant San Francisco restaurant with Richard.

She bought it, putting it on her credit card and ignored the financial analyst in her screaming that she had just blown her budget all to hell.

Wanting an immediate metamorphosis, she used the boutique's dressing room, changed into another dress she'd bought, tore off the tags, did her hair and dragged herself and her bags to a nearby restaurant. She dined in peace, but alone...and found herself remembering how much she loved this warm lively city. Why had it never seemed so romantic to her before? She smiled to herself, thinking of Richard.

It was dark when she headed back to J. B.'s office, and she was proud of herself for having resisted the urge to meddle further in her father's affairs.

But when she put down her bags in the hall to fish her keys out of her purse, her self-congratulation disappeared in a flood of guilt, panic and trepidation.

The door to J. B.'s office had been jimmied open.

She entered cautiously, making sure, as she suspected, that no one was inside. Light from the street angled in through the windows, casting an eerie glow over the quiet ransacked rooms. She flipped on a light. The drawers of Lucy's desk were open, files scattered on the floor, everything thoroughly, messily, searched. In J. B.'s office and his rooms the damage was worse. Chairs upended. Cushions askew. Papers everywhere. Even the personal contents of his closet and bureaus had been tossed around, searched. And his kitchen cabinets, his food, his refrigerator. A box of linguine had been spilled on the floor.

Holding the telephone with a dishcloth, Sheridan called Lucille Stein's home number. "Lucy...you're all right? You weren't here...."

"Sheridan?" Concern registered instantly in her voice. "I'm fine. What's wrong?"

"Someone's gone through the office."

"I'll be right over."

"No...no, that's all right. There's nothing that won't keep until morning." She looked at the destruction around her. No, there was nothing they could do to-night. "I just wanted to make sure you weren't here when whoever did this showed up."

"I wasn't," Lucy said with assurance.

Sheridan nodded absently. "I'm glad. I think...I should call the police."

"And tell them what?"

"I don't know. I...don't know."

She hung up and dialed a friend of hers in the police department, a Lieutenant George Davis. "Well, hello there," he said in his cheerful bass. "I heard you were back in town. What's up?"

"Someone's broken into J. B.'s office. I thought you might want to have a look around before I clean the place up."

"Me and a couple of lab boys will be right over."

While she waited, Sheridan resisted the urge to phone Richard. If she reached him, he would insist on coming over, and she didn't want that. Friend that he was, George Davis had a sharp, suspicious mind. He would want to know what a wealthy San Franciscan like Richard St. Charles was doing in J.B. Weaver's ran-sacked office. For the moment Sheridan didn't want to tell him, not until she heard from J. B.

A wiry, intelligent, red-faced, twenty-year veteran of the San Francisco Police Department, George Davis wasn't the least bit horrified by the mess in J.B. Weaver's office. He had seen it all before. "These guys were pretty thorough, weren't they," he said dryly. "Any ideas, Sheridan?"

"Me? No, uh-uh. I'm just home for a visit."

"Are you now?"

She pointed to her shopping bags. "I was out shopping when this must have happened."

"I see. And where's your dad?"

"Pop? Oh, he's out of town. On a case."

"Ah. Anything this might be related to?"

"I doubt it."

The lieutenant frowned. "Just want us to dust for prints and depart, huh?"

"I don't have anything for you, George. If I did, I'd tell you."

"Yeah," he said doubtfully. "Right. Know what these guys were looking for?"

"Petty cash, I would think."

"In a box of linguine?"

Sheridan prudently said nothing.

The lab boys did a cursory dusting for prints, gathered up their things and left. It wasn't that big a case: private investigator's offices searched. It happened all the time. Yet Davis lingered, his arms folded across his chest as he looked his menacing best. "Hear you've been seen around town with Richard St. Charles."

She smiled. "That's right. We met in Boston, but there's—we're just friends, George."

"He's just the kind of guy I've always pictured you getting mixed up with. He's the reckless type, you know. But I don't have anything on him."

"George, Richard St. Charles has nothing whatsoever to do with this mess."

He shook his head in despair. "Sher, Sher, you're good at skirting the truth, but you're terrible at lying. Always have been. If you need my help, you know my number. Okay?"

"Thanks, George."

"And this St. Charles character—if I were betting, I'd say he's all right. But I don't like to bet on things like that, you know?"

She nodded. "I understand."

"Good." And he left.

With a frustrating feeling of helplessness and that strange indefinable loneliness, Sheridan watched the police car pull out of its illegal parking space, wondering what she was going to do now. Her choices were limited, but clearly she couldn't remain inactive. In an effort to concentrate and blot out the mess around her and the questions it presented, she closed her eyes and bit down hard on her lower lip. *Think…you've got to think, Sheridan!*

Inexplicably, images of Richard St. Charles flashed before her. Images of a man who was strong, capable, understanding. Not images of a man who would ransack her father's office. That man simply and without a doubt was not Richard.

The thugs from earlier today? A whole new set of thugs? *Who?*

Her eyes flew open at the sound of footsteps on the stairs outside the office.

7

THEY WERE MOVING RAPIDLY. Richard? No. He always seemed to tread silently in his rubber-soled shoes.

She edged alongside the door, ready to pounce when it was thrown open. For the first time since she had landed in San Francisco, she felt prepared to handle whatever was dished out to her. Enough, she thought solemnly, was enough.

"Sheridan, it's me. Open up."

She relaxed her posture at the unmistakable sound of Richard's voice and opened the door. "Well," she said, "hello."

And then without any warning to herself or him she fell against his chest. He caught her up by the small of her back, holding her close as he surveyed the shambles of Lucy's office. He kicked the door shut. "Thought I saw the police," he murmured. "Sheridan...are you all right?"

She nodded and lifted her head off his chest. She would have extricated herself entirely from the embrace, except he still had hold of her. Of course, she knew dozens of ways to free herself. But she didn't feel trapped. She felt warm. Content. Not alone. She smiled at him. "I wasn't here when the damage was done," she said, surprised at the bitterness, even disappointment, in her voice. "I could have stopped them, found out what the devil kind of trouble J. B.'s gotten himself into this time... *Damn*, I can't stand this!"

"I know." He wasn't pitying or being superior, merely stating a bald fact. He rubbed the tense muscles in her lower back. "The time's passed for sitting back and waiting for J. B. to handle this affair on his own, hasn't it?"

Her eyes grew distant as she pictured her father, imagined what he would do if she were in his position: turn San Francisco upside down and inside out until he had her and some answers. "Yes," she said, "it has."

"Any idea who did this?"

"I'm betting D'Amours's men. Richard, he has to be behind all this somehow. That necklace opened some kind of can of worms for J. B. and D'Amours. A bigger can, I suspect, than J. B. intended. If he knew he was opening a can of worms at all." She groaned and threw up her arms; when they fell, they landed on Richard's outstretched strong forearms. "Dammit, I can't make any sense out of this. If the necklace is the problem, why search J. B.'s place? You're the one who has it."

Richard looked grim, his eyes shadowed. "Good point."

"Your boat...your house...they haven't been searched, have they?"

"No, not that I know of. From the looks of things here, I think there would be no question that J. B. doesn't have the necklace. Sheridan, maybe this is some kind of warning to him. Or us."

"Or maybe J. B. convinced them beforehand that he had the necklace, and they were looking for it, and—" She stopped herself, making two fists that had nowhere to land. "But why all the fuss over a five-hundred-dollar necklace?"

Richard smiled, not with levity, but with a tenderness Sheridan found reassuring. "We have all the right questions, don't we?"

She nodded. "Just none of the right answers."

"There's not much we can do now."

"No, there isn't," she said reluctantly. "I suppose I ought to clean up here. Lordy, what a mess."

Despite her protestations Richard insisted on helping. They pitched in together, beginning with the kitchen and working their way toward Lucy's office. They didn't try to sort out any of the mess, just got things up off the floor and somewhat back into shape. "Lucy has her routines for getting stuff back in order," Sheridan said. "She's used to this."

"And are you?"

"I've seen messes like this before here, but never without having an inkling as to why."

He smiled. "You've been away too long."

"Yeah, I suppose…." She caught herself. "No, dammit, this is part of why I left!"

"Sheridan, try as we might, we can't deny where we've been and where we're from. Roots and all that. Like it or not, this is your world."

She shoved a cushion back onto a chair. "Not anymore."

AFTERWARD SHERIDAN politely thanked Richard for his help. "At least I won't feel like I'm sleeping in the city dump," she said cheerfully, her mind trying to fight off her feelings, the ache that only appeared when Richard was near. The twistings and turnings within her that had nothing to do with her ulcer and everything to do with him. His self-evident maleness. The palpable sensuality that emanated from every inch of that tall solid body. Her mind failed at fighting off anything about him, which meant she had to get him out of there as quickly as possible. She walked over to the door and opened it. "Thanks for everything."

"Sheridan," he said, sauntering over to her, "I'm not leaving here without you."

She remained calm. "And why not?"

"Because anything could happen tonight, and I want to be here."

"Richard," she said smoothly, "I don't need your protection."

He, too, remained calm, but she could see the effort in the tensed muscles of his arms and the darkness of his eyes. "I'm not offering you protection. I'm offering you friendship. Companionship. If you're afraid of anything more, go into your father's office, toss me out a blanket and lock the door." His mouth twisted into an ironic smile. "Just look at it this way: if someone decides to pay you another visit, he'll get to stomp on me first." He moved closer. "Of course, it would make more sense for you to come and stay at my place."

Panic seized her. It was happening too fast, everything—the questions, the promises, the possibilities, the realities. Two days ago she was a contented, dutiful financial analyst with a problematic father. Who was she today? "I can't...."

Richard didn't push her. She could sense the control in him, but suddenly his eyes danced, and he grinned. "No linguine on the floor at my house," he pointed out, the teasing note in his voice diffusing her panic.

She was grateful. "True."

"And I have a guest room. Several, in fact. You can have your pick."

"Richard..." She sighed, kissed her finger and placed it on his lips. "You're perfect."

"I have been taught," he said, "all the rules of chivalry and sublimation." He laughed, offering his arm. "Come along. I believe the meter's run out on my white horse."

8

THE SCENT OF ROSES wafted in on a cool breeze through the open window, tickling Sheridan's nose as she rolled over in the big comfortable bed and snuggled up in the silk sheets and down pillows.

One eye opened and then the other, and all at once she was sitting bolt upright. It was 5:00 A.M., and she wasn't in the English country house of her dream. This was a dank San Francisco dawn, and she, Sheridan Weaver, could be her rational self again. She had to be. With the objectivity of a private investigator and the precision of a financial analyst, she considered her situation, where she was and what she was getting herself into.

She had to get out of here. Fast. Last night she had been panicky and shocked after finding J. B.'s place in a shambles, as well as disgusted with her inability to deal with her father's mysterious behavior. Richard had been there. Solid, attractive, confident. She had appreciated his control and his general, if reluctant, decency because last night she could have been persuaded not to spend the night in a quiet lovely guest room.

She would have gone to bed with him, no questions asked, none answered.

Which was not the way to find J. B. Not the way to get this business over with and herself back to Boston. Not the way to avoid emotional complications.

Richard St. Charles and Sheridan Weaver.... No, it simply couldn't be. She sprang out of bed and dressed in sleek pants and a cool cotton shirt. In Boston it would be eight o'clock. She would be drinking her second cup of coffee, reading the morning paper and listening to classical music on public radio. In a half hour she'd walk through the Public Gardens and the Common to work. She didn't have rosebushes outside her window or silk sheets, but it was a nice, fulfilling life. She made her own schedule and lived according to her own means. It was a life she didn't want to give up or jeopardize. Anything between her and Richard would be tempestuous, thrilling, but ultimately temporary. Even friendship. It had to be that way. He was that kind of man and lived that kind of life. She decided to leave him a note.

Richard: I have to handle this on my own. If you need me, leave a message with Lucille. Thanks.

Sheridan slunk out his front door, plucking a rose as she left.

She arrived at J. B.'s just before six, having enjoyed her quiet walk through the early-morning fog. She remembered the old days when she and her father would have breakfast together at their special coffee shop, and remembering made her feel as if she knew every nook and cranny in the city and half its population. This was her hometown as Boston never could be. She had grown up in San Francisco; she could be herself here.

Sheridan stopped these thoughts at once. What kind of seditious thinking was this? Absurd. She couldn't be herself here. That had been the whole point of leaving.

She took a long soothing shower and blamed Richard for her confusion and for the constant hypersensitivity of her skin. She had never been so aware of her body.

"Dammit," she muttered, toweling herself dry, "how am I supposed to concentrate on finding J. B.!"

As it turned out, she didn't have to. He was at the coffee shop and eating eggs and toast with Swifty Michaels. Sheridan plopped down on one of the chairs at the square table for four. "Well," she said sarcastically, "good morning."

J. B. glared at her. "Where the hell have you been?"

"*Me?* Me!" She turned to Swifty. "Do you believe this?"

Swifty shrugged. He was a short, wiry, intelligent man with iron-gray curly hair and few ambitions. He always looked the same, trouble or no trouble. Sheridan had known him forever.

"Well?" J. B. demanded.

"Are you two checking up on me?"

J. B. waved a hand, dismissing any accusation of overprotectiveness. He looked as refreshed and self-confident as always. "Sher, I know what you're like, and I know you're going to be sticking your nose where it doesn't belong."

"Like father, like daughter."

"Never mind the smart remarks, Sher. This is serious. I had to get some cash out of the safe and thought I'd check on you at the same time—only you weren't there. And the place was a wreck."

"You should have seen it before. I cleaned up."

"You weren't there when it happened?" J. B. snapped the question; Sheridan shook her head. "Then you're okay."

It wasn't a question, but Sheridan said, "Yes."

"You always could take care of yourself, Sher," Swifty said.

"Yeah, well, how come you two are here eating eggs if you thought I was in trouble?"

J. B. mopped up some yolk with a crust of toast. "I put two and two together, like always, and decided to give St. Charles a buzz."

"Oh, no."

"Yeah. I knew I was taking my life into my hands even conversing with the man over the phone, but I like to know where my daughter is—for my own peace of mind, you know. Anyway, St. Charles wasn't too thrilled to hear from me at 5:30 A.M., or any other time, I imagine. But I managed to get out of him that you'd spent the night at his place."

"In his guest room," Sheridan added.

"Of course. I'm sure he loved that."

"I was keeping an eye on him."

J. B. raised both bushy eyebrows.

Guido, the proprietor of the coffee shop, served Sheridan a cup of coffee and took her order for eggs. She had the feeling she'd better start her day with a good breakfast. "At five-thirty I was walking from St. Charles's over here."

J. B. drank some coffee. "St. Charles doesn't know that."

"I skipped out on him."

"Skipped out on St. Charles?" Swifty shook his head. "Dumb move, kiddo."

"I wouldn't talk about dumb moves if I were either of you," Sheridan retorted.

"This," J. B. said, "is getting uglier and uglier."

Sheridan leaned forward impatiently. "The question is, what are we going to do about this mess you're in? J. B., I need facts."

"Not this time, kid. Why don't you head on back to Boston before you lose your job?"

"I've taken care of that, J. B. I had some personal days coming to me."

"You could take St. Charles with you...."

"J. B., you're not listening to me!"

He ignored her. "Makes sense to me. How 'bout you, Swifty?"

"Makes sense to me, J. B."

Sheridan gave Swifty a disgusted look. "When have you ever disagreed with J. B.? Listen, you two, I am not—repeat not—going back to Boston, with or without Richard, until you, J. B., are acting normal again. Is that clear? And you can never mind my relationship with Richard St. Charles. It's none of your damned business! Now. I want to know what kind of trouble you've been stirring up with that fake necklace."

"Don't we all?" J. B. said.

"Not me," Swifty said. "I'm just having breakfast."

"At six o'clock in the morning? Come on, Swifty, this is a little early for you. But you and J. B. go back to the beginning of time. What's he having you do? Steal the necklace back from Richard because Vinnie or somebody has the heat on him? Did it ever occur to you two that you could just ask Richard for the necklace?"

J. B. sputtered into incredulous laughter.

"Sher," Swifty said gravely, "your pop stiffed St. Charles for a hundred grand. You think he's going to feel kindly toward J. B.?"

A shadow fell across their table, and they looked up at the white-shirted, gray-trousered, looming figure of Richard St. Charles. With his dark hair tousled and his jaw set hard, he looked as if he'd passed a bad night or, Sheridan amended, a bad early morning. She felt a twinge of guilt. Perhaps she had acted precipitously.

"I don't think," he said in his deepest, most menacingly quiet voice, "that I feel kindly toward any of you at the moment."

Sheridan refused to meet his eyes and said to J. B. and Swifty, "He has this knack for sneaking up on people. It's his rubber-soled shoes."

J. B. and Swifty gave Sheridan the kind of look that told her she was expected to handle the situation, which meant handling Richard. She tried an innocent smile. "Hello, Richard, won't you join us for coffee?"

"Yes," he said, "I will."

"Good move, Sher," J. B. muttered.

Richard pulled out a chair and sat. Swifty made a move to leave, but one look from Richard kept him in his chair. Guido brought Sheridan her eggs and automatically turned over the mug in front of Richard and filled it with coffee. Then he refilled everyone else's mug. No one thanked him, but Sheridan knew Guido would understand. He had known the Weaver clan and their propensity for tense situations for too long.

"Swifty," J. B. said, "I'd like you to meet Richard St. Charles. Richard, Swifty Michaels."

Richard smiled curtly at Swifty, and Swifty said, "I've won a lot of money on your horses."

"Legitimately?"

"'Course."

"Richard, my father and Swifty are respectable gamblers. If you're going to insult them—" His eyes bored into her, stopping her in midsentence. She clamped her mouth shut, then started again. "What do you want?"

"Cooperation," he said with deadly calm. "Honesty."

"A hundred grand," J. B. muttered.

Richard gave him a look that would have melted the Bank of America building. J. B. just shrugged and drank his coffee. Sheridan attacked her eggs. "I know how this must look," she resumed, "my being here with Swifty and J. B. at this hour of the morning, but we didn't meet here. It's just a coincidence. I've told you everything I know about this business, Richard. Anything else you want to know, get from J. B." She swallowed a mouthful of coffee and stood up. "Good seeing you again, Swifty. Pop, stay in touch, okay? Richard."

She turned, but Richard clamped a hand onto her wrist. She glanced down at him. "I wouldn't do that if I were you," she said mildly.

"Sit, Sheridan."

"Beg, Sheridan," she mimicked, annoyed now. "No. I'm leaving."

"Sher, for God's sake," J. B. said, waving his fork, "sit down. The last time you busted up the place, Guido threatened to call in the law." He smiled ingratiatingly at Richard. "I think I overdid the self-defense lessons, you know? Me, I'm satisfied with an introductory lesson in karate. Sheridan? She goes for her damned black belt."

"She's a compulsive personality," Richard said.

"Yeah." J. B. glared at his daughter. "Will you sit?"

Sheridan flounced back down into her chair, and Richard released her. His grip had totally disarmed her and not because it had been a particularly effective hold. Under ordinary circumstances she could have broken loose in half a second and not smashed a single one of Guido's unimpressive dishes. But ordinary circumstances would have involved a man she didn't like and a grip that didn't prompt images of lovemaking.

Under the table his knee rubbed against hers. She snatched her leg away, but caught his amused half smile as he sipped his coffee. *Damn the man*, she thought and looked to J. B. for help. J. B. shrugged. He, too, was at a loss.

Richard set his mug down. "J. B., how close are you to finding out what that necklace means to Vincent

D'Amours? It is D'Amours you've been chasing after—or running from—isn't it?"

"J. B. never discusses cases with nonclients," Sheridan said.

"Girl," J. B. grumbled, "when I want your help, I'll ask for it. How I stood all those years with you as my partner..." He turned his attention back to Richard. "The answer to your question is 'not close.' Look, if I explain, will you two drop this? Go to Tahiti or something and let me figure this out?"

"Maybe," Richard said. Sheridan made no comment.

"All right. Twenty-five years ago I was a professional gambler. So was D'Amours, only he always had more money than I did and took gambling far too seriously. It was never any fun for him—he's compulsive, probably needs help. Anyway, we were in a big game. The biggest damned game of my life. He put up a fancy necklace instead of cash, and I fell for the trick." J. B. sipped his coffee. "Like you did the other night, St. Charles."

"Perhaps I shouldn't feel like such a fool, then," he said mildly.

"Hell, no, you should feel like a jackass. I sure as hell did. And I was mad. God, I was mad. But there wasn't a whole hell of a lot I could do about it. And then my wife died, and I had a pesky toddler on my hands, and there just wasn't any more time to get even. I tossed the thing into some corner and got on with my life."

"How come I never saw the necklace?" Sheridan asked.

"Because I never showed it to you. It's not the kind

of mistake a person likes to advertise, you know? Anyway, when you left town, I started to think about finally getting even with Vinnie. I got myself into one of his games and won enough to make the evening worthwhile before I put up the necklace. I knew I was losing the hand and figured Vinnie must have known, too. So what was he going to say: 'Hey, J. B., you can't bet that thing, it's a fake!' I'd say, 'Yeah, you oughtta know, you cheat!' And he'd be stuck explaining to his hotshot poker friends. I figured he'd keep quiet, and he did. Except that your fearless St. Charles here offered me a hundred grand for the damned thing. How could I refuse?" He glared at Richard. "Didn't you *know* I was losing?"

"Poker is not my forte," Richard replied without embarrassment.

J. B. measured him with a look. "No, I guess not."

Sheridan, however, was more interested in facts. "So what did Vinnie do?"

"Collected his hundred grand, what do you think he did? By rights he should've been laughing up his sleeve at me—and St. Charles. Stiffed me twice in twenty-five years and stiffed one of the richest damned men in the city. Vinnie's kind of night, you know?"

"Instead," Richard said pensively, "Vinnie offered to buy the necklace back from me for a hundred thousand."

J. B. nodded, his weathered face grim. "Yeah. That's when I knew I'd hit a nerve."

Sheridan frowned. "Wait a minute. *Wait just a minute!* D'Amours offered to buy the necklace from you, Richard?"

"Yes, didn't I tell you?"

"No, you didn't tell me!"

Sheridan felt her blood pressure rising and her ulcer gnawing through her stomach. She gritted her teeth against the onslaught of pain and anger. "Damn it, Richard, if you'd told me, I'd have *known* D'Amours was behind this! And you, J. B. How can you possibly justify not telling me all this before? Dammit, I'm supposed to keep an eye on a millionaire as well as find my father, but does anyone fill me in on trivial little details like Vincent D'Amours's offering a hundred thousand dollars for a necklace he knows is a fake?"

J. B. groaned, disgusted. "What the hell's going on? Sher, I haven't told you a thing! How could I leave something out?"

"She's irritated with me, J. B.," Richard said, his voice unwavering.

That didn't assuage J. B. "Oh, for God's sake, what's this going to be? A council of war or a lovers' quarrel? Here, you two fight it out. Swifty and I got work to do."

"Do you need the necklace?" Richard asked.

"Why, you offering to give it to me?"

"I simply asked a question."

"I think you might be in danger so long as you have it," J. B. said. "Let's leave it at that."

"But you don't need it to conclude your investigation?"

"No. From the looks of my office, I'm guessing Vinnie thinks I've got it back—part of my plan. So it won't help if you decide to take him up on his offer to buy the necklace."

"I won't."

"How come you didn't in the first place?"

Richard gave J. B. a nasty tight-lipped smile. "At the time I thought it was worth a quarter million, not five hundred dollars."

J. B. turned to Sheridan. "There, you see? If I'd been on the level, if I'd been betting on the real thing in that game, I'd be out a hundred and fifty grand. It would have been worth a quarter million, and St. Charles would have gotten it for a mere hundred thousand. St. Charles, you got yourself a bargain. I should be mad at you."

"Your logic is incomparable," Richard said. "If this affair ends without my being reimbursed—"

"Reimbursed!" J. B. howled. "Sher, did you hear that? Listen, Mr. Hotshot, you got suckered. All you can do is be mad as hell. You can't get a cent off me. I knew that twenty-five years ago when I won the damned thing off Vinnie. I should've been more careful then, you should've been more careful now. That's the breaks, St. Charles. Chalk it up to experience."

Sheridan, who was getting used to Richard, wasn't amazed that he showed no emotion. He chose not to even comment on J. B.'s less than politic remarks. "In any event," he said calmly, "D'Amours hasn't repeated his offer. Should he, I won't accept—at least for the next two days. Sheridan and I will give you that long to solve this in your own way."

"Generous of you," J. B. said sarcastically.

Richard simply looked at him. "Meet us in your office at noon on Friday."

"What about you?"

"Sheridan and I will enjoy San Francisco and leave you to your own devices, unless you contact us for help. I can't see the four of us chasing down D'Amours together, can you?"

"If you've got the necklace, you could be in danger." J. B. was serious now.

Richard smiled. "But I'll have Sheridan. Together I think we can handle Vincent D'Amours."

Swifty muttered something about the two of them being able to take on a pen of mad bulls, and J. B. nodded thoughtfully. "I suppose. What if I don't show on Friday?"

"We'll assume D'Amours has gotten to you and act accordingly, probably beginning with a call to the police."

J. B. grimaced. "Friday, then." He flipped a few dollars on the table. "Here, kid, I'll buy you breakfast." He patted Sheridan on the cheek and stood up. "Wait till I get outta here before you start bouncing him off the walls, okay? Come on, Swifty."

While they were on their way out, Guido delivered a silent Richard St. Charles his breakfast while his taciturn companion debated which wall to bounce him off first. He buttered his toast. "I suppose you're angry with me for making a decision without consulting you."

She glared at him. "That's just for starters."

He smiled without mirth. "Imagine my anger at discovering an empty bed in my guest room and that idiotic note. I was willing to be in on this together, to work with you, but you chose to sneak around behind my back. Fine. I can be just as obstinate as you, sweet Sheridan. J. B. gets his two days, and you and I are going to present ourselves as a team."

"Is that an order?"

"It is what will happen."

"By the decree of a man used to getting his own way." She pushed her chair back. "I hope D'Amours comes after the necklace and takes you with it. Damn you, St. Charles, no one makes decisions for me! I am not an extension of you or J. B. or anyone. Goodbye."

He set down his butter knife. "Fair play's turnabout, Sheridan. But I've had my revenge. Now you know how it feels when someone you care about doesn't involve you in an important decision."

"Who says I care about you?"

"Sheridan, you're a stubborn, arrogant, impulsive woman, but I think I'll fall in love with you anyway. If you walk away now, it won't change anything. I am not easily deterred."

Slowly she turned, feeling warm, less alone and not at all angry. "So I've discovered."

She flagged Guido down and had her third cup of coffee.

9

"WHAT YOU HAVE TO understand," Sheridan told Richard that evening over a rich dessert at a popular Union Street café, "is that all my life it's been J. B. and me. We've always been a team."

Richard was leaning back in his chair, as relaxed and casual as ever, but attentive. "But in order to establish your own identity, you had to break up the team. You earned your MBA and moved out to Boston."

"J. B. encouraged me to go."

"Because he thought it was something you needed to do."

She nodded, picking at her chocolate cake. "No matter how hard I tried, I couldn't break away from him here. He's not an overprotective father—"

"I should say not. He did leave you to contend with two thugs."

"Oh, *that*." She shrugged dismissively. "No, J. B. has great faith in my professional skills, at least my investigative ones. I'm talking about being protective about my personal life. He has his opinions, of course, but he's never interfered with my choice of friends, neighborhood, entertainment."

"Lovers?"

His voice didn't change, but Sheridan could feel her body responding to him. She nodded. "Lovers, either. But they haven't been my chief preoccupation," she said, looking away. "I've often been too busy plunging myself headlong into the future, and it has never seemed to include a regular man, let alone marriage and settling down. I don't think J. B.'s ever minded that."

"You're not exactly ancient, Sheridan."

"Twenty-eight." She pulled her upper lip between her teeth and wondered why she was talking so openly about herself. She never had before, not with anyone, woman or man. Yet she couldn't stop herself. "My mother was twenty-eight when she died. It's peculiar being the same age she was then. I don't remember her at all. That's always seemed like some kind of betrayal to me, not remembering her. I've tried and tried, and I just can't. Sometimes I'll smell a perfume, something like that, and just get overwhelmed with emotion, sort of like spring fever, an odd mix of happy and sad. I don't know, it's probably just my imagination."

Richard pushed the remains of his cheesecake aside and ran a finger around the rim of his mug of cappuccino. "How did she die?"

"Car accident. I guess J. B. wondered if it might be connected to his profession, just gambling then. He checked it out, but it was just an accident. He's had women friends since then, but I don't think he'll ever remarry. And he's never put any pressure on me either way."

"He sounds like an ideal father."

"I suppose."

She held her mug of mocha coffee in her hands and looked out across the crowded café. It was situated in a narrow building and decorated in a captivating mix of Victorian and clean contemporary, with the desserts and assorted goodies on display under glass. She wasn't watching Richard, but knew instinctively that he was watching her. All day they had stuck together, pretending it was a normal day and they were an average man and woman. By mutual agreement they didn't discuss the necklace or J. B....or what would happen when the two days were up. Or even what would happen during the two days, beyond trying to cooperate and stay together. Instead they went shopping downtown for some clothes to further pad Sheridan's wardrobe, now that her stay in San Francisco continued to expand. She didn't know whether to blame Richard, San Francisco or herself, but she had gone straight to the bright cottons and fresh pastels, to clean lines with style and grace. Tonight she wore a turquoise skirt and top, with her hair hanging down and pulled off her face with two turquoise combs.

"We're a family, J. B. and I. There's no getting around that. And we were tied together professionally for a long time. I worked for him on and off through college, then joined him full-time when I graduated. He's taught me everything about the business."

"But you wanted out."

"I don't know if I wanted out or just didn't want to be my father, to live the life he's lived. It's not a bad life, but I felt as if my choices had all been reduced." She paused, choosing her words carefully, not for Richard's sake, but for her own. "I don't like having people think I'm another J.B. Weaver. I don't want to be everything to him. I don't want to *be* him. So when I got the opportunity, I got out. I left him high and dry, Richard. He needs a partner, but he hasn't replaced me. He acts as if he's thirty-five still, and—and, dammit, he makes me so mad sometimes! I mean, why did he have to drag out that damned necklace and go after D'Amours? Hasn't he got enough to do?"

"It seems your leaving town liberated him in a way, too, from a daughter he obviously adores."

Sheridan scowled. "J. B.'s always done exactly as he pleases."

"Then why do you feel so guilty?"

"Because I'm not who he wants me to be! It wasn't easy to leave, but I have my own life now, and I'm not coming back here. I'm not going to get sucked up in his world again."

"Even if you risk denying who you are?"

She glared at him, his half smile only adding to her irritation. "I am *not* denying who I am. Remember the woman you met at United Commercial? *That's* the real me. The bona fide, tried-and-true Sheridan Weaver."

Her outburst had no visible effect on Richard. He said calmly, "Then what I've been seeing here in San Francisco is a mirage."

"That's as good a word as any. Yes, a mirage."

He laughed softly. "I've never made love to a mirage, but yesterday—"

"I thought we weren't going to discuss that."

"You didn't look like a mirage," he went on relentlessly, "or feel like one...or taste like one."

His tone, his words, his shadowy eyes, all combined to make her tingle from the roots of her hair to her toes. How could she pretend she didn't want him? It was no good telling herself this other Sheridan Weaver, this brash daredevil, was the one who wanted him. She had wanted him in Boston, too. "You're never alone when you're a schizophrenic," she muttered, then looked up at Richard. "You're not making this easier."

His smile reached his eyes. "What am I not making easier? Being two people? No, I should hope I'm not making that any easier. Dividing yourself into a West Coast and an East Coast personality, a Before and an After Sheridan Weaver, is a lot of nonsense."

"I knew I could count on you to be understanding."

"Understanding, yes. But not sympathetic. Establishing a life apart from your father is one thing, but you're carrying it too far. You're afraid of me, of what's happening between us, because you're afraid of being yourself."

"Richard, haven't you been listening? I'm afraid of *not* being myself!"

"You select certain traits—such and such is this Sheridan Weaver, such and such is that Sheridan Weaver. Then you act accordingly, depending on which Sheridan Weaver you are trying to be." He leaned forward, no sympathy etched on the hard lines of his face. "Only every now and then you forget all your stupid rules, and we get to see the real Sheridan Weaver, the one who's the nutty, talented private investigator *and* the intelligent, methodical financial analyst. And that's the Sheridan Weaver that intrigues me. That's you, love. Try to deny it, and you'll fail."

"You're so sure?"

"Yes."

"Why?"

"Because I've been watching you."

She twisted her mouth from one side to the other thoughtfully, wishing she had kept their conversation light and impersonal. Richard St. Charles was beginning to know her too well. He was beginning to see possibilities she wasn't sure she wanted to acknowledge: a Sheridan Weaver who was neither J. B.'s wild daughter nor a stodgy businesswoman, but both. She had never met anyone who could accept her as both.

"It's an interesting idea," she said finally. "I'll give it some thought."

"And in the meantime?"

She grinned. "You'll have to keep watching, I guess."

He leaned back and gave her a sly rakish look. "My pleasure."

WITHOUT FANFARE or discussion Sheridan decided to spend the night at Richard's house. By staying she knew she was tempting fate. Or more accurately, herself. Neither time nor distance nor willpower would lessen her attraction to him. Even if she left now—not just returning to J. B.'s place, but returning to Boston and leaving her father and Richard to their own devices—she knew she would still wake up nights, feeling the way she felt now. She had never been so aware of her senses and her emotions, how connected they were. Simply put, she was falling in love with Richard St. Charles.

They stood in the hallway that night, not touching, in no hurry to go to their separate rooms. Sheridan could feel the certainty rising inside her; yes, she wanted to spend the night with him. Not just here in his house. But *with* him. In his room, in his bed.

"Can you get through this, Sheridan?" he asked softly. "Another night not knowing where J. B. is? If it were my father—"

"But it's not. J. B.'s a professional, Richard. He's been up against worse than Vincent D'Amours, but we don't really know what kind of pressure Vinnie's under. If he cracks, someone could end up getting hurt, and not just my father. I think you could be in danger, too, Richard."

"And you."

"I'm not worried about me. All I have to lose is my job, my father, you." She was deliberately flippant. "I guess I've grown kind of attached to you the past few days—you know, like a big brother."

Maddeningly he said nothing. He didn't even smile. He merely watched her as she ran a hand self-consciously through her hair. "Believe it or not," she said, "I've said dumber things in my time. Well, I've been up since five o'clock, and I'm beat. I'll just…" Her voice trailed off.

He continued to watch her, his eyes hooded. "Your room is exactly as you left it."

"I…"

"Good night, Sheridan." He turned away.

"Richard!" He looked back at her, and she smiled briefly before growing serious, not nervous, but aware, very aware, of what she was thinking and feeling and wanting. "Richard, what do you want? Now, I mean. Tell me. Please."

He didn't move, but she could feel the heat emanating from him, the hunger. "You." His voice was husky. "Sheridan, all I want is you."

Still she held back, unable to go to him, unable to speak.

"I'm not asking for any promises, Sheridan," he went on quietly. "And I don't want to push you into anything you're not ready for. I only want to make love to you now, tonight."

"Richard…" She moved toward him, gliding, as if through a fog, and reached him, felt his strong arms slip around her, his lips on her cheeks, then her mouth, until she was breathing in the scent of him, responding, aching.

"Let's go upstairs," he whispered into her mouth.

She smiled, took his hand, kissed it and then kissed his mouth. They walked up the stairs together. There was no weakness in Sheridan's knees, and only the fluttering of longing in her stomach. She had no doubts. Because all she wanted was Richard St. Charles.

His room was all gleaming woods and beiges with clean lines and open spaces, as frank and sensual as he was. Sheridan didn't feel the least bit strange or out of place. She felt at home. As if she belonged.

"Sometimes," she said as she sat on the edge of the wide bed, "I feel as though I've known you forever, and yet I actually know very little about you. Tell me, who is Richard St. Charles?"

He smiled. "A man who finds Sheridan Weaver fascinating and lovely, talented and zany—"

"You're talking about me, not yourself."

"You know me, Sheridan." He was serious now. "What you don't know are details. I want you to know them. I want you to see where I work, meet my family, wander through the fields and hills of my farm, explore everything I own. I want all that to happen, but that's not what's important between us." He came to her and sat down beside her, only their thighs touching. "I want to be a part of your life, Sheridan, and I want you to be a part of mine."

"That's what I want, too…I think."

But she could say no more. Richard draped an arm over her shoulder and pressed his lips into her hair; she could feel him breathing in the scent of her. With a deep, aching sigh she placed her hand on the wall of his chest, smiling up into his eyes. "I've never known anyone like you," she managed to say, her voice hoarse, different even to her own ears.

"Good," he murmured, bringing his mouth down. His tongue outlined her lips, slowly, erotically, and she was lost to the myriad sensations evoked by caressing him and having him caress her.

"I want to touch you everywhere," she said, not bold, not pleading, but stating the truth.

He pulled off his clothes, moving quickly, unabashed. His body was browned and hard, she noted with pleasure as he lay down alongside her. There was a small smile on his lips, but she saw the need in his eyes. "Please feel free to touch...."

Sheridan knelt beside him and ran her hands over his entire body, exulting in the feel of every hair, every muscle, loving the hardness of his skin under her fingertips, the changes in texture, the signs of his own brimming passion.

And then he shuddered, and she could feel under her hands the desire rippling through him. He didn't remain still for long. He wrapped one long arm around her waist and brought her down beside him. "Your turn," he murmured and went for the buttons on her top. Yet she could see he was showing great restraint. Judging by the tension visible in his fingers, the intensity in his eyes, she knew he would have preferred to rip off her top. She didn't blame him. She wanted it to be gone, nothing between them.

Before the thought was formed, the top was cast aside, and Richard was tackling her bra. Her skin felt cool in the air of the shadowy room. "Sometimes," she said, her voice choked with emotion and longing, "I can't really remember what my life was like before I met you. It's only been a few days, but..."

"It seems like a lifetime," he said, completing her thought, and smiled into her eyes. "I know."

The job was complete then, her clothes scattered, nothing to bar his touch. He whispered her name and placed tiny feathery kisses on her eyelids and cheeks, until his mouth came to hers and opened, his tongue plunging between her lips, circling, probing. They both quaked with a hunger that was almost palpable. "You feel so right, so good." As his hands traveled down her body, even his voice was a caress.

"You don't have to say anything." She wrapped her arms tightly around his lean waist, wanting to pull him into her now, forever. "Just love me."

"All night and all day, darlin'," he breathed, and she could feel the primitive, encompassing tension within him. "All our lives."

She moved against him, her slender body trim from years of hard physical exercise, yet soft and trembling with want. Instinctively she knew they both were ready. Ever since they had met, this moment had been ordained, and when her legs parted and he plunged into her pliant warmth, she cried out with the newness of his body in hers, the pure physical excitement of it. At the same time she felt as if she'd come home, as if she had found a place in him, with him, where she belonged, a place she knew and adored and wanted to be. They were gliding together through a sunset of light and flashing color: cool lavenders, gentle pinks, warm oranges and bright searing reds. Their bodies were molded, pulsing with the rhythm of time, their souls merged, one not absorbing the other, but sharing, each making the other whole, vivid, vibrant.

Soon they were no longer gliding. They were flying, skidding through the moonlight, reaching out for the stars. Closing her eyes, Sheridan saw only the bright pure light of her love and the boundless joy and energy of her passion, until there was that single flash, brighter than light. Together they cried out with wonder and fulfillment and lay still.

It was a long time before either spoke. Richard stirred first, opening his eyes, as soft and incandescent as she had ever seen them. "I don't ever want to lose you, love," he said quietly.

"Richard—"

He pressed her lips shut with a kiss. "Nothing about your two selves now. Please. Let's just enjoy the moment."

"I am." She smiled and touched the hard line of his chin. "As I have no other."

SHERIDAN AWOKE EARLY in the morning and slipped out of bed, not daring to touch the slumbering hulk of a man beside her, for she knew if she did she would have to touch him some more, awaken him, kiss him, make love to him. And today was a different day. She didn't regret what she had done. There would be no unforeseen consequences; they were responsible adults and had seen to that. But she didn't go for one-night stands, and neither, she believed, did Richard. Which meant their friendship had taken a decidedly intimate turn. Last night emotions and physical needs had prevailed; it was right that they should have. Today she had to rein in her emotions, control her physical desires and consider what she was letting herself in for. A love affair with Richard St. Charles. Or something more?

Clearly decisions had to be made. She had to sit Richard down and discuss their relationship. That was a must. Before they landed in each other's arms again, certain parameters had to be established.

But there would be no talk and no decisions until she had J.B. Weaver safe in his office and back to work.

With a look of longing, of pure sexual hunger, Sheridan left Richard sleeping and went downstairs, carrying with her the image of the browned well-defined muscles of his naked shoulders and back and that mass of wild dark hair.

She found her things in the guest room, showered and changed into slim-cut linen pants and a bright raspberry silk shirt. In a carefree gesture she wound her thick hair into a single braid trailing down her back.

She felt terrific...until Richard wandered into the kitchen wearing nothing but a dark-brown terry-cloth bathrobe. The bathrobe, she had a feeling, was purely for her sake. With a pang that penetrated to the pit of her stomach, she recalled all that had passed between them the night before.

"'Morning, Sheridan," he murmured, pouring himself coffee. "Sleep well?"

"Like a rock."

He smiled. "Did you?"

When he sat down, his robe opened at the front, revealing dark hair and a stretch of hard chest muscle. It was all Sheridan could do to keep from groaning aloud.

His hair was more tousled and wilder than usual, prompting visions of him in bed, his face above hers in the shadows, his kisses. Looking at his long brown feet, she recalled the tingles that had shot through her when his toes had climbed up her bare legs.

He sipped his coffee. "Something wrong?"

"Uh-uh." She licked her lips and warned herself to keep the conversation brisk and professional. One personal remark from him and there was no telling how she'd react. "I was thinking about running by the office this morning, seeing if Lucille has anything for me—us. Since you're, um, not dressed, why don't I go and meet you back here?"

"You could always just call."

"No, I'd rather just run by. Okay?"

"Fine, but you know you don't need my permission."

"Right, that's true. I was just…making conversation." She shot up from her chair. "Give me an hour or so."

He eyed her with some amusement, as if he could tell exactly what was going through her mind. And, more to the point, through her body. She was flushed, trembling, burning with a desire so sudden and so intense that she wasn't sure an hour's jaunt to J. B.'s office would temper it. Obviously self-restraint wasn't doing her a damned bit of good! Why not go ahead and make love with the man? He wanted to; she wanted to.

"Bite your tongue, woman," she muttered.

"Sheridan, for heaven's sake, sit down," Richard urged. "I'm not going to attack you."

"You're right. I'm acting like an ass." She sat. "But I

do want to run over to J. B.'s. Richard, I have to do something. I'll go crazy!"

He smiled. "I understand. I think I'll run by my office this morning. I haven't stopped in in quite some time."

"Ah-ha," she said, amused. "So the loose and hip Mr. St. Charles does work, after all."

"Only when the spirit moves me, sweet Sheridan. I'm not the workaholic you are."

"I'm not a workaholic," she countered. "I have excellent work habits, a routine that allows me to get done everything I need to. I even pencil spontaneous time into my schedule—Richard, what are you laughing at?"

"How the hell can you schedule time to be spontaneous?"

She sniffed, caught. "I could pitch you out on your ear—"

"Or you can admit I'm right. You shouldn't always opt for violence when someone sees through you, love."

"I just call it spontaneous time. I suppose free time would be more accurate. You would understand if you ever worked."

She was just teasing, but unexpectedly his eyes grew distant. "I used to work and damned hard, too. I'd be in the office by seven and out, on a good day, by nine—and come home and work until midnight. It wasn't much of a life. But I wanted to build what my family had given me into something of my own, something I could be proud of, that they could be proud of, too. I wanted my parents to know I cared and that I was honored to be a St. Charles, to have what I'd been born to.

The best way to do that seemed to be to make more money." He settled back in the chair, stretching out his long legs. "I was wrong."

"They didn't appreciate your efforts?"

He looked at her. "They knew I was working hard, but they didn't know I loved them. In those days it seemed as if I loved only myself. And maybe I did, I don't know. It doesn't matter now. I finally discovered the best way to let someone know you love them is to say so. My life-style was killing me, and it was turning away people I cared about. So I changed."

"Just like that?" She could hear the doubt in her voice, but she couldn't believe Richard was a man who changed easily.

"It was difficult at first, in some ways like ending an addiction. But I knew I had enough money to last a lifetime, and I could run my businesses with a trusted staff. I haven't retired, but I could. Knowing that has made it easier to pull back. I don't want to own the world, Sheridan. I realized I most want to *see* the world, experience it and, if I can, leave my mark one day, not by adding to my net worth, but by doing something worthwhile. I'm not sure yet what that is."

"You're a man of many sides."

"People are like that, Sheridan. Most are, anyway. We're complex and contradictory. If we weren't, life would be dull. I don't spend a great deal of time analyzing myself. I try to accept what I can and change what I can't."

She nodded solemnly, thinking not only of him but of her.

"So you see," he said, a glint of mischief in his eyes, "I'm not just the careless playboy who dropped a hundred and some odd grand at a high-stakes poker game."

"But you enjoy your fun."

"I enjoy my life." He drank some of his steaming coffee. "We all have certain duties, though, and mine is to let my staff know I'm still alive. Why don't you meet me at the yacht? I won't be long. We can have lunch and go for a sail around the bay. What do you think?"

"I don't know. I hate to leave in case J. B. needs me."

"We won't go out, then. Leave my number with Lucy. Or would you prefer to stay here?"

She frowned, thinking. "Let me see if Lucy has anything for me."

Richard laughed, both with amusement and understanding. "It's hard for you to sit on the sidelines, isn't it?"

"Not your style, either, I wouldn't think."

"True." He set his mug on the table. "You'll be all right, won't you? You won't do anything crazy—and you'll be careful?"

She looked at him. "No, I think I'll just be my reckless, impulsive, cocky self and get into trouble—"

"Sheridan," he warned.

"I'm sorry. But you don't have to worry about me."

"Why, is it too confining to have someone care about you?" He didn't raise his voice; it was still even, controlled. "Sheridan, I'm not asking you to give up your independence or your sense of self. I'm only asking you to be careful."

She smiled tenderly, remembering the joy and delight

of their lovemaking and the sense of freedom she felt with him. "I'll be careful if you will."

"Of course. I'm always careful."

And they both laughed.

Sheridan went straight over to J. B.'s office, where Lucy was fussing and fuming over the mess the search party had left her. Yesterday had been her day off, but she'd stopped by, assessed the damage and come in at seven the next morning. "It's one way to keep the files up-to-date, I suppose," she grumbled to Sheridan. "You hear from himself?"

"Yes, as a matter of fact." Sheridan sat on the floor next to Lucy, who was lining up papers in little stacks in front of the file cabinet. Sheridan told J. B.'s secretary everything.

"Damned fool," Lucy said. "Should have left well enough alone. There's a message on your desk, by the way. It was on the machine."

Her desk? Sheridan went into J. B.'s office, and there, on her old desk, was a "while you were out" slip efficiently filled out. She chuckled and grabbed the phone to return Miriam Knight's call.

Miriam answered on the first ring. "What's up?" Sheridan asked.

"Humph. That's my line, Sher. The grapevine has it you've been seen around town with St. Charles. What gives?"

Sheridan smiled, not at all surprised word had already gotten to Miriam. Miriam was like that. Either she gravitated to gossip or gossip gravitated to her, but she always managed to hear things. "Nothing. We just share a professional interest."

"In what?"

"I can't say."

"I heard he lost a pile in a poker game with Vinnie D'Amours. Your pop was there, too."

"How do you know?"

"Oh, word gets around."

"Especially when you're nosy and ask a lot of questions," Sheridan said good-naturedly. "Miriam, please, leave this alone for a while, okay? I'll let you know when the story breaks."

"All right, all right. I'm just impatient, I guess. Things have been quiet around here. Keep me posted, will you? And you and St. Charles…if you need a sympathetic ear, I'm here, you know that."

"Thanks, Miriam, but there's no need to worry."

Miriam grunted. "I'll bet. Keep in touch, okay?"

Sheridan padded around the quiet office for an hour, sharpening already sharp pencils, peering out the window, straightening a paper clip and bending it back again. Thinking about J. B. Richard. Herself. Finally Lucille had had all she was going to take. "Go do something," she said. "You're driving me crazy."

"I'm worried about J. B."

"Sharpening pencils down to the nub isn't going to help."

Sheridan sighed. "I suppose."

"Sheridan, he'll be all right."

"How do you know?"

"Because he always is."

"I'd still feel better if I were *doing* something. Having lunch aboard a yacht while J. B. is locking horns with Vincent D'Amours doesn't seem right somehow." Especially, she thought, when lunch was with Richard St. Charles. "Well, I guess I don't have too many choices—"

The telephone rang. Breaking form, Lucy picked it up on the first ring and said, "Weaver Investigations…yes, she's right here." She handed the receiver over. "For you."

"Richard? J. B.?"

Lucy shook her head.

It must be Agnew looking for a way out of some crisis, she thought, taking the phone. "Sheridan Weaver."

"Welcome back to San Francisco, Ms Weaver," said the silky-smooth voice of Vincent D'Amours.

Her ulcer began to burn, but she kept the tension out of her voice. "Thank you, Mr. D'Amours."

"Working for J. B. again?"

"No, just visiting."

"Having a good time, hmm? I didn't think a lady dick would go for a playboy like Richard St. Charles—or that he'd go for you."

"Lady dick?" She laughed, just managing not to sound derisive. "Only you, Vinnie. Now what can I do for you?"

"That's the question I've been waiting for. I've got a simple painless job for you, Sher."

His pause left her enough time to tell him she hated sleazes like him to call her Sher, but she said nothing. As J. B. would have put it, the ball was in D'Amours's court.

"Interested?" he asked.

"Perhaps."

"You heard J. B. dropped a necklace in a poker game with me, didn't you? St. Charles ended up with it. Don't pretend you don't know, Sher, because everyone in town knows J. B. tells you everything."

She frowned and caught the wide worried eyes of Lucy on her. Poor Luce. How had she stood all these years of life with the two Weavers? "Quit beating around the bush, Vinnie. What do you want?"

"The necklace."

"What makes you think I can help you?"

Vinnie laughed, a thin, nasal, nasty sound that rattled Sheridan's composure. "I know you, pretty lady. I've played poker with you, remember? You can help—we both know it."

"I don't have the necklace."

"St. Charles still has it, then. Fine, it doesn't matter to me as long as you can get it."

"Mr. D'Amours," Sheridan said coldly, "I have no intention of doing anything of the sort—"

"That's where you're wrong, pretty lady. I got a great way to persuade you: J.B. Weaver."

She gripped the phone, her knuckles turning white, and instantly Lucy was on her feet. "Go on," Sheridan said hoarsely.

"A couple of my boys found him nosing around. I figured you might trade him for the necklace."

"That's kidnapping, Vinnie."

"It's survival, Sher. Call me when you can meet my

terms. This doesn't have to be unfriendly. Your father for a paste necklace? Come on."

"Dammit, I don't have the necklace!"

Vinnie remained infuriatingly cool. "Then get it." He hung up.

Lucy took a deep breath. "Sher?"

"It was Vinnie...." She raised her eyes and met the other woman's anxious knowing gaze. "He's got J. B., Lucy."

10

IT WAS ALL SHERIDAN could do to keep Lucy from chasing after Vincent D'Amours herself, but she managed to get the ample secretary to unroll her sleeves and calm down. "If anyone calls," Sheridan told her, "I'll need you here." *J. B. will*, she added silently.

"Are you calling the police?"

"I don't know. Vinnie didn't make any explicit threats...."

Lucy humphed. "J. B. sure as hell isn't staying there of his own free will!"

"I know."

She went into J. B.'s office and sat at her old desk, trying to put all the pieces together. There had never been any doubt that Vinnie wasn't a nice man, but would he go so far as to kill J. B. over a five-hundred-dollar necklace? Why would he even risk a kidnapping charge? How could she even be sure Vinnie wasn't bluffing, that he did have J. B.?

What does the necklace mean?

"First things first." She grabbed her bag, dug out her three-by-five note cards and looked up the number to St. Charles Enterprises.

First she wanted to talk to Richard. Not because he had the necklace, but because she loved him and wanted him with her.

The crisp professional voice of a receptionist answered. "I'm sorry," the woman said, "but Mr. St. Charles is unavailable."

"I'm sure he'll talk to me—it's an emergency. My name's Sheridan Weaver."

"You don't understand, Ms Weaver. Mr. St. Charles is not in the office today."

"You mean he's not there yet?"

"We don't expect him today at all, Ms Weaver. May I leave a message for when he does come in?"

"No." Remembering it wasn't the receptionist's fault that her boss was a snake in the grass, Sheridan managed to thank her before hanging up.

Unavailable! Not expected today!

So much for trust, honor and consideration. A man like that, a woman like her—it was impossible. They were both too stubborn and independent. They'd fight all the time.

"And never tire of each other," she murmured to herself.

Unless Richard was in cahoots with D'Amours, after all, which would be tiresome, indeed. She shook off the thought at once. Not only did she not in her heart believe such a scurrilous thing, it wasn't logical. If Richard and Vinnie were in this together, Vinnie wouldn't need to kidnap J. B. to force Sheridan into getting the necklace for him.

Grabbing the phone, she punched out Swifty Michaels's number. "Swifty? It's Sheridan. Have you heard from J. B?"

"No."

"What do you mean no? I thought you were helping him out."

"He changed his mind."

There was something in Swifty's tone that Sheridan had never heard before and didn't like. He, too, was worried. "Did he say he'd be in touch?"

"Friday noon, same as when he said he'd see you."

"Then he did go after Vinnie alone? *Damn.*"

"Sher...what is it?"

"J.B. Weaver is a stubborn man, Swifty, but this time that trait could hurt him. Swifty, Vinnie's got pop."

J. B.'s longtime and stalwart friend took a moment to digest this news before asking succinctly, "What're you going to do, Sher?"

The burden, she thought, was on her shoulders. At worst she felt like a businesswoman with an MBA and twelve kinds of vinegar. At best she felt like a rusty P.I. She spoke slowly, choosing her words carefully. "I'm going to call George Davis," she said and swallowed. "Then I'm going over to Vinnie's. I want to talk to him, see for myself...I have to do something, Swifty."

"How about St. Charles?"

Her heart lurched, then sank. "If you hear from him, tell him—tell him I don't like liars."

"Sher?"

She could hear the concern in Swifty's voice. "I'm

okay, Swifty," she said, feeling the tears spring to her eyes. *Hell, I am okay. I have to be!* "I'll get J. B. out of this mess. I've done it before."

"If you need me—"

"I've got your number."

Instead of calling Davis herself, Sheridan had Lucy do the deed. Davis would try to talk her out of going to Vinnie herself. But she'd been in this position before. She knew what to do, what J. B. expected of her, she hoped. "Tell him I'm on the case, and I'll call him later."

"But—"

"And if St. Charles calls, tell him lunch is off."

Sheridan swung her bag over her shoulder and stalked off, feeling more than ever like the Sheridan Weaver of old: competent, confident, daring…and alone.

SHE REMEMBERED THE WAY to Vincent D'Amours's estate. It was located in Marin County, the house itself constructed well up into a steep hill. It was all glass and wood, spectacular, with a dramatic view of the bay. But Sheridan had never liked D'Amours, and she figured one benefit of a major earthquake would be to send Vinnie's little castle crashing into the bay.

Still, she didn't think he was a murderer. He wouldn't be pushed into killing J. B. He was a cautious man—a paranoid or a realist, Sheridan wasn't sure which—and had made his grounds as impenetrable as modern technology could. There were the ordinary safeguards: ten-foot spiked wrought-iron fences, security men, a guard at the main gate, Dobermans prowling the property. In addition, Vinnie had installed a computerized security system that he bragged about at poker games.

J. B. had always said that, if pressed, he could get inside D'Amours's estate without so much as a Doberman blinking an eye. Sheridan had never doubted him.

Until now.

Sliding her car onto the shoulder of the road ten yards from the main gate, she had to consider that J. B. had tried...and failed. Somehow D'Amours had found out what J. B. had been up to; now her father was his old nemesis's prisoner.

There was no other word for it: prisoner.

She shuddered, turned off the engine and climbed out of the car. If she could talk to Vinnie, appeal to his reason, his gambler's honor...something. But surely J. B. had tried all that. Too much was happening too fast: her father had been captured by what he would simplistically call "the bad guys"; her lover had lied to her; and she was back in the messy, dangerous, exciting world she had rejected. She was trusting instinct and rusty skills. Or operating on them, at least.

Sheridan slammed the door shut; as she expected, a voice rang out, "Hey!" The two men she had encountered at the yacht club ran toward her and, when they recognized her, stopped abruptly, just out of striking distance. They drew their guns.

"For heaven's sake," she said, "put those things down. I want to talk to Vinnie. There's no reason we have to resort to violence."

The blonde waved his gun. "Out."

They were pre-verbal, she decided. She spoke slowly. "I want to talk to the boss."

The dark one waved his gun. "Out."

"We're not making any progress. Vinnie expects me to call him—"

"Then call."

This was from the blonde—two whole words together. "Amazing," she said. "I'd prefer to talk to him here."

"No talking," the blonde said.

"Out," the dark one said.

"You'll tell Vinnie I stopped by?" She regarded them with her best supercilious look. "Me Sheridan Weaver." They just stared at her, guns pointed. She shrugged and pulled open the car door. "Oh, and tell J. B. I'm on the case, okay? You're feeding him good, I hope. He's allergic to peanut butter."

They started toward her, but she hopped in the car, turned the key and was off. Obviously she wasn't going to get to talk to Vinnie, and she wasn't one to flog a dead horse. As she did a U-turn in front of them, she smiled and waved.

If she'd brought her gun, she could have shot them both, stormed the estate and rescued J. B. Or, more likely, gotten them both killed. Black belt or not, Sheridan preferred an approach with far more subtlety and finesse.

"If only I could think of one," she muttered, cruising back down to Sausalito.

She drove past the yacht club, gripping the steering

wheel hard as image after image of Richard and last night battered her mind, her senses, her emotions, like so many waves washing over an empty, isolated beach. Even if she tried, she couldn't shut him out. Yes, clearly he had lied to her. But surely he deserved the chance to explain. Walking out of his life now wouldn't be fair to either of them. If he was a liar and a cheat, if last night had been nothing to him but a physical release, then better to have that out now, to open herself up to deeper but cleaner wounds.

Reminding herself that she wasn't the type to run away from a problem, Sheridan parked between a Jaguar and a Mercedes and ran all the way down to the dock, where she grabbed a tanned blond college kid who worked at the club. "Hey, slow down," he said, grinning. "Take it easy...."

She caught her breath. "I need a ride out to Richard St. Charles's yacht. He's expecting me." *If he's there,* she added silently.

"Okay, will do. A party brewing out there or something?"

Sheridan looked confused. "Not that I know of. Why?"

They got into the small launch. "Saw a boat come up a little while ago—there, it's still there."

Bobbing in the water alongside Richard's yacht was a small speedboat. It was empty. Sheridan could feel her defensive instincts grind into gear, but she didn't pale or tremble. She merely grew very, very wary. "Did you see who was in it?" she asked.

"A couple of guys, maybe three."

"Is Richard on board?"

"'Course. We would've done something otherwise."

"Then he welcomed them? They appeared friendly?"

"Yeah, sure."

If they had had guns held close to their chests, their backs turned to the club, an indifferent party on shore wouldn't necessarily have noticed if they had forced their way on board.

"Something wrong?" the boy asked.

"I don't know, but I didn't think Richard was expecting guests other than me."

"I can go out, check around, if you want. Hey, relax, I won't let anything happen to you. The name's Peter, by the way."

Sheridan decided to indulge him. "Thank you, Peter."

Unless she was wearing her *judogi*, the special pants and jacket used for martial arts practice, and her black belt, people tended to underestimate her ability to defend herself. Often that worked to her advantage. But if these were more of D'Amours's men, there was a good chance they already knew all about one Sheridan Weaver. Having a young healthy ally couldn't hurt. If something had happened to Richard—

No. She wouldn't think that way. She couldn't.

The launch sputtered to a stop alongside the yacht, behind the speedboat, but Peter left the engine idling while Sheridan climbed to her feet.

For the second time that day she cursed herself for not having packed a gun. She hated guns, though J. B.

had insisted she learn how to use one. Not everyone, he claimed, was impressed by flailing arms and legs; in their business a gun was a must. J. B. and Sheridan both considered violence of any sort a last resort, even a sign that they'd made a mistake somewhere along the way.

Just then three men leaped into the speedboat, all armed, none Richard. Peter swore under his breath and sat down quickly, ready to make his exit—and Sheridan's for her. She clapped a hand on his shoulder. "No, wait!"

He looked around at her, panicked. "But they have guns!"

"Yes, but—Oh, God."

The speedboat roared to a start, but Sheridan paid no attention. They were hired muscle; there wasn't a thing she could do even if she could catch them, which she knew she couldn't. She had always had a good sense of her limitations. Nevertheless, with J. B. a captive, she might have tried something—some trick, some ruse, she didn't know.

The sight of Richard changed all that. He was leaning over the side of the yacht, and blood was pouring down his face.

"Richard!" she yelled.

He waved a hand. "I'm okay."

"I'm going aboard," she told Peter, her voice a hoarse whisper. "You can go on. There's…there's no need to call the police. I'll—"

"Fine, fine, no police. Hey, I'm easy."

And afraid, Sheridan thought, but this was no time to try to explain. As soon as she was on the yacht, Peter swung the launch around and took off. Sheridan hoped he was afraid enough *not* to call the police, simply because she didn't want to take the time to answer their questions.

She raced to Richard and grabbed hold of his upper arm, steadying him. He had an ugly gash on his forehead, along his hairline above his right ear. From experience Sheridan knew he had been pistol-whipped. Under the circumstances she was relieved.

"Thank God you're all right," she managed, gasping for air as the tension and fear of the past few moments was released. Her stomach burned. She needed a glass of warm milk, her father to be safe…Richard.

His black eyes focused on her. "I do not feel all right, thank you. Where the hell have you been?"

"I could ask you the same. Here, let me have a look—"

With a glare he pushed her hand aside and stumbled over to a deck chair, which he plopped into before glaring at her some more. And swore. And dabbed at his cut with a muted-blue sleeve. Sheridan pulled up a chair and sat next to him. He needed to cool down. She understood the pain and humiliation of having a handful of arrogant, mindless goons beat him over the head. What she didn't understand was why his wrath had to be directed at her. After all, *she* should be angry!

"Why didn't you go after them?" he demanded.

"Wonder Woman I'm not. Richard, you need some ice for that cut. It'll start to feel better in a few minutes, and—" She stopped herself from delivering another platitude. "If it's any comfort, I know how you feel."

He shifted abruptly. "No, dammit, you don't know how I feel! You don't know what it is to care for someone, do you? No, better yet, you don't know what it is to have someone care for you."

She scowled at him, both in confusion and disgust. Bloodied or not, he had no right to be yelling at her. "I'm not the one who hit you. Look, why don't I get some ice. Maybe it'll improve your mood."

"Sheridan." The low, rough voice kept her in her seat. "Where the hell have you been? I expected you to be here. You weren't."

"As you say, fair play's turnabout. I expected you to be at your office. You weren't."

He stared at her. "What?"

"I called St. Charles Enterprises, and you weren't there."

"No, I wasn't. I—" His eyes narrowed, intent and alert, almost as if the bloody wound wasn't there to plague him. "Why did you call?"

"First tell me why those men were here."

"They were looking for the necklace. They said they had you."

Sheridan was confused. "Had me? What do you mean?"

"Had you. Kidnapped, captured, stuffed in a trunk, strung up by your toes—had you." He swore, dabbing at his cut with the back of his hand.

"And you believed them?" She scoffed. "Really, Richard."

He moved too suddenly—probably, she thought,

going for her throat—and swore with vehemence at the pain that resulted. "Woman, you weren't here!" That was as vociferous as Richard St. Charles ever got. "You said you'd meet me on the yacht, and when there was no sign of you, I— Dammit, what the hell was I supposed to believe?"

Good point, she thought, pensively rubbing the tip of her thumb along her lip. "Interesting," she mused. "Interesting."

"What the hell is so damned interesting about thinking the woman you love has been carted off by a bunch of goons?"

The woman you love. She looked at him, feeling warm and confident and not alone. "Richard, this is all getting complicated. I'm sorry you were worried about me, but there were mitigating circumstances that I'll go into in a moment. First tell me what happened here. Please."

He sat back, calmer now, the blood coagulating around his gash, and considered her request. "All right. From the beginning. I came by about twenty or thirty minutes ago." His voice was low and steady. "When I didn't find you here, I called Lucille and my house in the city—needless to say, without success."

Leave it to Lucy not to give out any details.

"I wasn't worried," he went on. "I assumed you'd gotten restless and had gone off on some lark of your own and would return in due time. I settled down to wait. Then company arrived."

"The three men."

"Yes. They came aboard with guns drawn and demanded the necklace. I decided to feign both innocence and ignorance, which didn't work."

"Not easily believed where you're concerned," Sheridan put in dryly.

"I told them I didn't keep track of worthless fakes and hadn't the slightest idea where it was."

Sheridan winced. "Is that when they hit you?"

"No, that's when they told me they had you, and if I didn't come up with the necklace, they'd do harm to you."

It was precisely the same deal Vincent D'Amours had offered her for the return of J. B. Did that mean Vinnie didn't have J. B., either? She regarded Richard thoughtfully. "Did they indicate they were acting for D'Amours?"

"No, but I assumed they were."

"I see. So what did you do?"

Richard gave her a small wry smile that, despite his battered state and her own worries, sent waves of emotion and warmth undulating through her. "They were considerably more specific about what they meant by 'harm.' Like a fool I jumped them. *That's* when they hit me."

"I'm touched, Richard."

"It was damned silly, wasn't it?"

"Impulsive, not silly. At least they didn't kill you."

"Then they'd never get their hands on the necklace, would they?"

"You didn't give it to them?"

"Presumably they were about to beat its location out of me, but you came swooping to my rescue and scared them off." The lightness of his tone didn't match the seriousness of his expression. "I probably would have thrashed them, despite being outnumbered and under siege, once I found out you were safe."

She remembered J. B.'s sarcastic words: "your fearless St. Charles." Yes, he was. "So you should be grateful. You're alive, I'm alive."

"Woman," he said, resting his head back against the chair, "if one thing in this world is irrefutably true, it's that Sheridan Weaver is alive. It's the Weaver charm, I'm sure, that lends you such vitality."

"I hope it still works for me," she said quietly.

Richard eyed her. "What does that mean?"

"It means I received much the same ultimatum from D'Amours about J. B. He called this morning and said he had J. B. and would return him for the necklace, which I was to get from you by hook or by crook—unless you were willing to take him up on his offer of a hundred thousand dollars."

"And?"

"And I believe him. I have no reason not to, Richard. I called Swifty, and he hasn't heard from J. B. Even Lucille's worried. What happened here certainly casts doubt on whether D'Amours does, in fact, have J. B., yet I can't operate on the assumption that J. B. is safe." She twisted her hands together. "You were the first person I called, Richard. Only you weren't where you said you'd be."

"I know." His voice was gentle and tender. "I didn't lie to you, Sheridan. I had planned on going to my office, but on the way I was thinking about that necklace and what it could possibly mean to a man like Vincent

D'Amours. It occurred to me that if we found out that much, we might stand a chance of sorting out this mess. So I detoured to my bank, got the thing out of my safe-deposit box and took it over to a jeweler I know. He identified the owners of the original."

Sheridan stared at him. "You mean there is an original?"

"Most definitely. It belongs to Peter and Amelia Livingston. They live in Pacific Heights. I haven't been in touch with them. I came directly here to talk with you and decide what we should do."

"I guess I shouldn't have jumped to conclusions, huh?"

He smiled, no longer belligerent, and got painfully to his feet. "I guess not. Though trust doesn't come easily, does it?"

"No, but it does come."

She rose and followed him below, where she ordered him to sit down and be still while she doctored his cut. "Tell me what you did after D'Amours called you," he insisted. "I can't imagine Sheridan Weaver sitting still while her father could be in danger."

She had hoped to avoid any mention of her unproductive visit to the D'Amours estate, but at the same time she wanted to hold nothing back from Richard. With a warm facecloth she cleaned off the blood around his cut while she told him everything, including her remarks and thoughts on Vinnie's choice of thug.

"Slipped right into your P.I. mode, didn't you?" he said with a grin.

With the cloth tucked around her fingers, she was

gently moving closer and closer to the gash itself. "Not necessarily," she said.

"I'm sure you're not that flippant with a United Commercial vice president."

"No, but I can think the remarks, at least."

"Which is why you have an ulcer."

"Life with J.B. Weaver is why I have an ulcer."

"Ouch!" He swore. "If you're going to maul me, perhaps I should take over."

"Sorry. I don't think you have a concussion."

"A black belt, an MBA and now an MD."

"Do you want to see a doctor?"

"No." He seized the cloth and finished the job himself. "You shouldn't aggravate me while I'm working."

"I'll remember that in the future. I'm not squeamish about these things, love, but your touch leaves something to be desired—at least right now. You do, however, have your moments." He reached one long arm out, grabbed her by the waist and brought her down next to him. She started to sink her head against his chest, but he touched her under the chin with one finger and tilted her chin up to him. "I never felt so lost," he whispered, "as when I thought those cretins had gotten hold of you. I'm so very glad you're alive, Sheridan Weaver."

Her lips parted as his mouth covered hers, bringing warmth and sensuality into her, joy and light. He touched her breast, his fingertips just grazing the nipple, and in spite of all her concerns, all her questions, she could feel the ache of her response. "Me, too," she murmured.

He smiled into her eyes. "I suppose J. B. would have our heads if we made love while he languished in some dank cell of D'Amours's. What do you say we have a chat with the Livingstons?"

11

PETER AND AMELIA LIVINGSTON lived in an opulent
house on Vallejo Street with a dramatic view of the bay.
They were an elderly couple, well dressed, formal and
polite. Sheridan and Richard were invited to join them
in their rose garden for tea. With a graciousness and ease
that surprised Sheridan, Richard accepted. This, she
thought, was a world in which he was comfortable. But
was there a world in which he felt awkward and ill at
ease? He seemed perfectly content to accept whomever
he happened to be with, not because he was insecure
about his own identity, but because he was very, very
secure. She would have to give all this some thought,
but later. After they learned about the Livingston necklace…and located Jorgensen Beaumont Weaver.

Tea was served by a uniformed maid in a small but incredibly elegant and beautiful garden. Sheridan noted a
decidedly unexpected but alluring rope hammock in the
far shady reaches of the garden. She pictured herself cur-
ling up there, enjoying a warm San Francisco afternoon.

She could do the same on her rooftop deck in Boston,
she reminded herself.

"Mr. and Mrs. Livingston," Richard began, "thank

you for agreeing to see us on such short notice. As you've perhaps inferred, this is a matter of great importance to us."

Sheridan raised an eyebrow as she tilted her china teacup into her mouth. How different Richard seemed now, compared to that first morning at United Commercial! She remembered quite well his brusque approach to her, a perfect stranger.

The Livingstons both assured him that the meeting posed no problem at all and urged him to continue.

"Ms Weaver is a private investigator here in San Francisco."

"Why, yes, of course!" Amelia Livingston cried. She was a tall slender woman with pale-blue eyes and silver curls. "You must be J.B. Weaver's partner. His daughter, I believe?"

Peter Livingston chuckled. "My wife is an avid fan of mysteries, in fiction and in real life."

Hence the hammock, Sheridan thought. Now she could picture Amelia Livingston curled up there. "Yes, J. B.'s my father," Sheridan replied.

"I've followed his—and your—exploits in the papers. Several people we know have retained your agency's services over the years. Nothing sordid, you understand."

"Of course," Sheridan said smoothly.

Amelia set her cup and saucer in her lap, an eager look in her eyes. "Please, go on."

Richard, who had yet to touch his tea, proceeded. "Some years ago—twenty-five, I believe—Mr. Weaver came into possession of a necklace that is reputedly a copy of a necklace in your collection. I would like you to look at it and tell me if this is the case."

The energy and excitement went out of Amelia Livingston's face; she glanced quickly over at her husband, a good-looking man of about her height with a paunch and a receding hairline. His look was equally troubled. "Certainly," he said.

Keenly observing what was going on, Sheridan sat back quietly while Richard removed the fabled fake from the inner pocket of his muted-gray jacket and passed it to Amelia Livingston. Together she and her husband laid the black velvet case on the table and opened it.

And together they gasped.

"Oh, Peter," Amelia Livingston moaned and sat back heavily in the wicker chair.

Peter Livingston rose and began pacing on the stone terrace. "I'm not sure where to begin," he said.

"This is a copy of the one you own?" Richard asked.

"Yes. Yes, it is."

For a moment Richard said nothing, but Sheridan could see he was measuring the situation, what to say and not to say. "Mr. and Mrs. Livingston, J. B. won this necklace more than two decades ago during a poker game. At the time he was a professional gambler. He had expected the necklace to be a valuable piece of jewelry made with real stones, not paste. Circumstances, however, prevented him from pursuing his loss, so he put the necklace away. Recently he retrieved it, placed it in a game with the same individual from whom he had won it all those years ago…and I ended up with it. We have reason to believe this necklace presents a dangerous situation for J. B., for us and, apparently, even for its original owner."

Amelia Livingston scoffed at this, raising her hand unconsciously to an antique cameo at her throat. "*We* are the original owners!"

Sheridan sat forward. "Of the copy, too?"

"Yes."

"You're both too young to remember," Peter Livingston said. "Twenty-five years ago our house here on Vallejo Street was burgled, our entire collection of jewels stolen…and our housekeeper, a charming, intelligent girl for whom we felt a keen responsibility, was killed."

He paused, letting his words soak into the minds of his two guests. Sheridan felt herself growing rigid. This was all much, much more serious than she had hoped. Why couldn't the issue have been some silly vendetta between J. B. and D'Amours? But grand larceny? Felony murder?

Mrs. Livingston resumed the grim tale. "The thieves, I'm sure, thought they were getting away with millions of dollars worth of gems, but they weren't. My husband's father, who began the collection at the turn of the century, was an eccentric, suspicious man. He had every piece copied by a skilled jeweler, and while they're not worthless and hold a certain sentimental value for us, they're not remotely as valuable as the original pieces."

"The perpetrators have never been caught," Mr. Livingston went on. "It was said that the infamous Bernard was the mastermind behind the operation—an embarrassing muddle for him, I'm sure—but there's never been any proof of that."

Glancing over at Richard, Sheridan saw that she didn't have to explain about Bernard, an international jewel thief whose image was far from romantic. If violence was deemed necessary to obtain results, he used it. Sheridan greeted the news of his possible involvement in her father's troubles with grim acceptance, yet found herself wanting to touch Richard, hold on to his hand and share his strength of spirit. A week ago such a longing would have sent her screaming into the night, fearful of losing her own strength of spirit. Now she acknowledged it, wanted it, relished it.

With a jerk of his wrist Peter Livingston gestured at the necklace on the table. "Until now none of the copies has surfaced."

"It couldn't be a coincidence?" Sheridan asked. "Another copy?"

He shook his head. "No, I'm afraid that's unlikely in the extreme. The copies my father had made were extremely precise and probably wouldn't be detected as fakes by an amateur, at least not immediately. Anyone trying to imitate the work would need either the original or the copy itself. The genuine pieces of the collection have always been kept in our safe-deposit box. Since that night twenty-five years ago, they've never seen the light of day. It's an appalling waste of such skill and beauty, I'm afraid, but we just can't bear to wear any of the pieces while Maria's murderers walk free."

"I understand," Richard said quietly.

"Do either of you know Vincent D'Amours?" Sheridan asked.

"We know of him," Mr. Livingston said, "but we've never met him. Why?"

"If it's all right with you," Sheridan continued, "I'd like to get to the bottom of this before we give you any of the details, but if there's any chance Maria's murderers can be brought to justice, we'll do what we can."

Amelia Livingston sighed sadly. "It was such a waste. Such a horrible, tragic waste. For what?" The question hung unanswered in the warm scented air.

Thanking the elderly couple for their hospitality and their willingness to dredge up painful memories, Richard and Sheridan promised they would keep in touch.

At the front door Richard turned suddenly. "Mr. Livingston, Mrs. Livingston—would you be willing to sell the genuine article?"

Even Sheridan was caught off guard. *What now?*

"As far as I'm concerned," Mrs. Livingston said with feeling, "you can have the whole bloody lot, but they're not mine."

"Amelia, of course they're yours as much as mine," her husband chided her; obviously this was an old bone of contention.

"It's the Livingston collection, not the Amelia Sanders collection. Peter, you must decide."

He smiled. "My wife is stubborn."

"That's something I can relate to," Richard said with a broad, friendly grin. Sheridan and Mrs. Livingston exchanged long-suffering looks.

"Forgive me for sounding like one of the novels my wife reads, but do you believe having the original will help you locate this Bernard fellow or whoever was responsible for that dreadful crime all those years ago?"

"It's possible," Richard said, "but I can't make any promises."

"I could loan you the necklace."

That made more sense to Sheridan, but Richard was already shaking his head. "That's very generous of you, Mr. Livingston, but I would prefer to use the original only if you were willing to risk losing it. By loaning it to me, you're indicating you want it back. That's too complicated. If you sold it, I would then be able to do with it as I pleased."

Sheridan frowned. What the hell was he talking about?

"I *will* promise you, however," he went on, "that if I am still in possession of the necklace when we conclude this business, I'll sell it back to you."

Peter Livingston rubbed his thumb along the edge of his sharp chin, giving the matter some thought. "All right," he said finally, "all right, I'll sell it to you. What are you willing to offer?"

"This morning I talked with a jeweler here in town." He named a name that the Livingstons responded to with murmurs of approval. "I asked what the genuine version of the copy would cost in today's market, and he said it would vary depending on the quality of the

stones. The highest-quality gems would earn a maxi-
mum price tag of three hundred thousand dollars. I'll
assume your necklace is of the highest quality and offer
you that amount."

If Sheridan had to guess, she would have said Peter
Livingston hadn't a clue as to the dollar value of any
piece in his collection. "Fine," he said, "but now the
necklace will be yours. I—we—don't want it back. One
woman has already died because of it. We'd feel better
if it can be enjoyed by someone else." His eyes rested
on Sheridan, but she stepped back, suddenly embar-
rassed. Richard was coming up with the money for the
necklace; it would be his.

The two men retreated to the dining room to make
the appropriate phone calls and close the deal. Mr.
Livingston made arrangements to go to the bank to re-
move the genuine necklace from the safe-deposit box.
Richard and Sheridan accompanied him.

WHEN THEY LEFT THE BANK, Richard was humming to
himself, the sun catching the highlights in his dark hair
and the sculptured lines of his face. Sheridan scowled
up at him. "That's twice in less than two weeks that
you've bought yourself a necklace without having it
appraised."

"Ah, yes," he said, a jaunty spring to his step, "but
this time I have a plan."

Although they were both keyed up and anxious to
put the plan into effect, come what may they had to eat
so they drove out to Sausalito for a very late lunch at the

club. Before Sheridan could ask how Richard felt about having the two necklaces on him with only himself and her for protection, the manager pulled him aside, undoubtedly to discuss with him certain "irregularities" witnessed on his yacht. She ordered herself a beer and watched Richard smile that devastating smile. Within seconds he had the manager smiling and nodding. Sheridan wondered what Richard had told him.

Richard returned to the table and dropped into a chair opposite her. "Hanging around you has made me remarkably glib," he said. "I have a feeling he thinks I'm an undercover narcotics agent."

Sheridan laughed. "As J. B. says, whatever works." But mention of her father made her solemn again, and she drank her beer, thinking of what the Livingstons had said. "If D'Amours can be tied to that heist twenty-five years ago, he could go up for felony murder. There's no statute of limitations on that, and all he had to do was be there. He didn't have to kill that poor maid. He just had to help the people who did." She licked the foam off her lips. "Which means J. B. just might be in more trouble than I thought—except somehow I still can't believe Vinnie would actually kill anyone himself or even willingly be a part of something like that. He always survived by his wits. Crude force wasn't his style."

"It sounds to me as if he got himself involved with the wrong group of people twenty-five years ago."

"And now he doesn't want to pay for it. And J. B.—"

"I think he knew what he was getting himself into," Richard said.

"You're right." She smiled suddenly. "Never underestimate J.B. Weaver—or so he told me all his life. I can't
let my worries fog my thinking. He'd disown me. You
said you had a plan. I want to hear it. As I see things,
we have to force Vinnie's hand—but without hurting
J. B., wherever he is."

"That's the sticky part, isn't it?"

"It usually is," Sheridan said dryly.

Richard nodded. His hair was tousled, blacker than
ever, as were his eyes, deep and endless, mesmerizing.
The bandaged cut above his right eye had drawn looks
from fellow club members, but no questions. He didn't
invite idle chatter or look as though he would tolerate
nosy questions. Sheridan was impressed—not that she
was deterred. From the beginning Richard St. Charles
hadn't intimidated her. She would always ask him anything she wanted to ask, and he could answer her or not.

Perhaps that was one reason they were drawn to
each other: she was no more threatened by him than he
was by her. She loved him for who he was. He didn't
have to change to suit some arbitrary list of do's and
don'ts for the perfect man.

Leaning over the table, Richard outlined the bare
bones of his plan. Sheridan listened, offered sugges-
tions, arguments. They batted their ideas back and forth,
compromised on some points, stood fast on others, until
finally they reached a consensus: they had a plan, and
it was worth a shot.

It was Richard who slipped his coins into the pay
phone and called Vincent D'Amours. Sheridan paced in

front of him, forward two steps, backward two steps. Forward, backward. And listened intently.

"Ah, Mr. D'Amours, I see you're answering your own phone today. Expecting an important call, are you? Well, my man, this is it. Richard St. Charles here. Are you paying attention? Good. I'll only say this once. I have in my possession two necklaces from the Livingston collection...." He paused and winked at Sheridan: he'd hit a nerve. "Please don't waste my time with arguments. I've made the connection between you and that nasty episode twenty-five years ago, but it means nothing to me. Ancient history. Oh, is that so? Well, I might be willing to believe you didn't kill that poor girl. I have two necklaces, however, that undoubtedly could tie you to a felony murder charge."

Forward, backward. Sheridan kept moving; she had to.

"Yes, I've heard you have J.B. Weaver, but I'm not interested in an even trade. Here's what I propose. We'll play poker tonight, at your estate. I'll come with no cash, just the two necklaces. You have J. B. If he goes free, I'll play the necklaces. But first he walks out of there— Wait, that's not all. The genuine necklace is worth three hundred thousand dollars, and I'm not sure we can place a dollar value on the fake. What's your freedom worth, Vincent? I'll tell you what it's worth to me: a million dollars. That's what you'll have to put into the pot before I'm willing to throw in *either* of the necklaces." He paused, reaching out and snatching Sheridan by the waist, pulling her close. "Well? Good. I'll see you tonight, nine o'clock."

He hung up and kissed Sheridan once, hard, on the mouth. "Sweetheart, either that man's a compulsive gambler or he's working on a plan of his own."

"Or both."

"Did I sound convincing?"

"Absolutely. After seeing you put up a hundred grand for the fake to begin with, I wouldn't be surprised if Vinnie believed you—not that it matters, remember? According to our plan, you shouldn't have to go through with that game."

"Of course…but it would be fun to beat that bastard at his own game."

"Richard!"

"Don't think I'm a match for him, love?"

"Not at the poker table. He'd skin you alive."

"You could give me pointers…."

"In five hours? Even you're not that slick, St. Charles." She hooked her arm through his. "Besides, we've got work to do."

DRESSED IN a loose-fitting black *judogi*, her dark hair knotted tightly at the back of her head, Sheridan crawled into the rear well of Richard's Porsche. It was a tight fit for her long body. She glanced at her watch: eight-thirty.

"You look like a damned maniac in that outfit," he told her.

"Good, maybe it'll scare them off if they come after me."

But they both knew the main purpose of the garment

was to permit her to move quickly and silently through the estate, without, she hoped, being seen. While Richard was dealing with Vincent D'Amours, she would be looking for her father. Neither she nor Richard believed for a moment that Vinnie would just turn J. B. loose.

Richard arranged a blanket over her, then tossed a few paperbacks, files and a box of tissues on top of that.

"What do I look like?" she asked from the claustrophobic confines of the blanket.

"The back of a car." She could sense his grin.

"St. Charles…"

"Have a fun ride. You're sure you want to go through with this?"

She didn't hesitate. "Of course."

They had been over every conceivable detail, discussed everything that could possibly go wrong and planned their reactions. But no matter what happened, Lieutenant Davis had agreed to give them one hour, no more, no less. At ten o'clock the police would present a warrant to search the estate of Vincent D'Amours. If no one had located J. B. by then, they would.

It was only a hunch he was even there. As Sheridan had explained to Davis, D'Amours hadn't been a model of efficiency and logic thus far.

Davis himself had been less than thrilled to hear her story. "I knew you were acting weird," he had muttered. But he had dug out the file on the Livingston case, listened and contributed his thoughts on the evening's escapade. "It's a damned harebrained scheme. Sounds like something J. B. would come up with."

In the end he had agreed to help.

The Porsche started and, with the smell of mothballs in her nostrils, Sheridan curled herself up and felt the car negotiate its first curve on the way into the Marin hills.

"While you're stuffed back there and don't dare move," Richard said cheerfully, "I'm going to tell you something, Sher."

"Richard, you're not being fair!"

"No, but you know the saying: all's fair in love and war."

Her heart pounded. "And what's this?"

"Love, Sheridan. Sweet unending love. I'm in love with you. I think I have been since I saw you frowning over those printouts—damn, it seems like months ago. But no matter. I've always known it would be like that, with the right woman. We're both stubborn and independent, but with each other we don't have to pretend to be anything else."

"But, Richard…"

He didn't hear her. "There's time, Sheridan. I'm not asking you how you feel about me. I'm telling you how I feel about you." The car dropped down a gear as it sped up a hill. "And I'm in love with you."

"With me, Richard? Or with the P.I. Sheridan Weaver you've gotten to know during the past few days? What will you think when I turn back into a financial analyst?"

But most of her words were lost in the blanket and the sounds of the engine, and they finished the trip in silence.

THE CAR SLID to a smooth halt, and a male voice said, "Just have to make sure you came alone, Mr. St. Charles."

"As you wish." Richard's tone was even, noncommittal. "But you won't need that gun."

Sheridan appreciated the warning, although it was no surprise to her that Vinnie's men were armed. Scrunched up in the well of a Porsche, she was at a distinct disadvantage. She remained very still and, using her years of training, breathed slowly, steadily and silently. Her eyes were open. Even through the thick blanket she could see the beam of the high-powered flashlight.

"Satisfied?" Richard said, the light still on her.

"What's this junk back here?"

"You answered your own question."

Sheridan admired Richard's cool. She and Davis hadn't been convinced that Richard had the experience to pull off his scam but, as the lieutenant had said, three hundred thousand dollars and his hide at stake would help, "not to mention his ladylove." But Sheridan hoped Richard wouldn't jeopardize himself on her account. His "ladylove" could take care of herself!

"Okay, go on in," the guard said. "Park out front and use the front door."

Without responding Richard edged the Porsche along the smooth driveway. Sheridan had drawn a diagram of the estate, but couldn't vouch for its accuracy. As much as she had never liked Vinnie, this she had never planned for.

The engine stopped. In the silence Richard whispered, "We're parked directly in front of the main entrance of the house, but on the other side of the driveway, under a tree. If you get out on the driver's side, you won't be seen. Are you all right?"

"I'm fine. Richard…" She swallowed, unable to bring herself to say she loved him. She did. It was that simple, yet there were so many complications, so many uncertainties. "Be careful."

"I will."

"Remember: Vinnie goes for a straight whenever he can."

"I hope the game won't get that far, but it's too late for any coaching, darlin'. We're on."

With a click of the door he was gone.

Sheridan closed her eyes and, mentally removing herself from her surroundings, counted slowly to one hundred. Richard would be inside now, greeting Vinnie, showing him the five-hundred-dollar necklace Vinnie had deemed worthy of so much ugliness. And why not? It linked him to a murder.

That was number one on Davis's list of things they should remember. Richard had touched his wounded forehead and said he wouldn't forget. He'd already sacrificed three hundred thousand dollars to find the killers of that young woman.

When she reached two hundred, Sheridan pulled off the blanket and rolled into the driver's seat, ducking under the windows. She refused to let her imagination run riot. It was a cool, clear evening. The shadows of the trees danced eerily in the light from the house.

Sheridan cracked the door open, slithered out into

the dark shadow of an oak and, crouched down, crept alongside the car. Through the floor-to-ceiling windows she could see D'Amours, in a formal black suit, pouring liquor from a crystal decanter. He was a small, slim, mean man who dyed his hair black and wore rings. J. B. had never trusted men who wore rings.

Richard stepped forward, accepting the drink. Even from a distance Sheridan could see that his movements were measured. His fluid body and expensive casual clothes radiated self-confidence and a certain fearlessness. Vinnie just tried too hard. Beside Richard, D'Amours looked incompetent, even ridiculous.

Which, of course, he wasn't.

As Richard and Sheridan had anticipated, D'Amours wasn't immediately forthcoming with one Jorgensen Beaumont Weaver. Until he had the fake necklace— and, knowing Vinnie, the genuine version, too—Sheridan knew he wasn't going to let J. B. go free. This wasn't Vinnie's style, not in poker, not in life.

Compulsive gambler that he was, he would play Richard's game. But there wasn't a chance in the world that he was going to let Richard St. Charles walk out of there with a million dollars and both necklaces. In Vinnie's mind the only question would be whether or not Richard would need some arm-twisting to cooperate. Once Vinnie had the copy safely in his hands, he would destroy it and any evidence of his role in the unhappy events of twenty-five years ago.

Then he might consider releasing J. B.

In the big house the two men sat at a polished round

table, and Richard, giving in with a show of frustration, laid the necklaces on the table. Sheridan could recall every detail of their timeless design: diamonds alternating with emeralds, all set in gold, until, at the center, they met in a cluster dominated by a single exquisite emerald.

Vinnie examined the pieces. Then he pushed a deck of cards toward Richard, and Richard cut them. He was buying Sheridan some time.

One hour.

She bit her lip. *If I were D'Amours, where would I stash someone like J. B.?*

Without a sound she slunk through the shadows along the perimeter of the driveway, avoiding another look at the gaming table. Sheridan made her way to a side entrance of the house. The door was locked, but down the hill and perhaps thirty yards from the house were a garden house and a smaller toolshed. She almost grinned. Of course. D'Amours wouldn't keep J. B. in the house if he could possibly avoid it.

There was a sidewalk, but she skirted it and, resisting the urge to run, moved silently among the uneven shadows cast over the lawn. The blond heavy from earlier that day was standing guard in front of the toolshed. Hesitating only a few seconds, Sheridan appraised the situation.

Then she sprang out from behind an oak. The man swore in surprise as he saw the streak of black coming at him, but Sheridan disarmed him with a slicing blow and, when he came at her, flipped him and landed a kick that would render him unconscious for the minutes she needed to free her father.

She grabbed the stray gun, fished some keys out of the thug's pocket and opened the door.

"Hey, kid," J. B. grinned wanly, "I've been expecting you."

"Oh, J. B." She hugged him and quickly explained what was happening.

"St. Charles is in there with Vinnie? Vinnie'll chew him up and spit him out. Hell's bells, you two are impossible."

"He can handle the situation, J. B."

J. B. grunted doubtfully. "It didn't occur to you that Vinnie might have plans of his own?"

"Of course he does, but Davis will be here at ten. That only gives Richard another..." She glanced at her watch and winced. "Another forty-five minutes."

"St. Charles could be shark meat by then," J. B. muttered, straightening. "Sounds like it's going to be a hell of a game, if Vinnie hasn't cleaned him out already."

"I gave Richard a few pointers before we left. He may not be a great poker player, but he has other strengths."

J. B. eyed her. "Yeah, I'll bet."

"You know about the Livingston collection?" Sheridan asked sharply, turning away from J. B.'s probing look.

He was disgusted. "What do you think I've been doing the past week, sitting on my hands?" He swooped down, grabbed the stray gun and gave Sheridan an encouraging hug. "Come on, let's go see if we can mess up Vinnie's life some more."

In his T-shirt and jeans and with no apparent damage to his person, J. B. strutted off toward the house. Sheridan caught up with him. At the side door they tried the keys on the key chain; the third one worked. The door opened into a spacious den. Down a hall they could see lights and hear voices.

"Has he got any goons in the room?" J. B. whispered.

"Not that I saw. Richard wouldn't have agreed to play until the room was cleared."

"Good thinking. How long did you put the guy outside down for?"

"Ten minutes tops."

"You're too kind, Sher."

They headed off down the hall, Sheridan feeling like her old self again, J.B. Weaver's partner. It was both unsettling and comforting. She and J. B. needed to work together now, think alike, trust each other. But where would that leave her tomorrow? She had worked so hard to be able *not* to think like J.B. Weaver.

The casual, sandpapery voice of Richard St. Charles reached to where they stood in the hall. "I'll take two cards," he said.

It was an innocuous statement that meant nothing, but nevertheless, Sheridan found herself catching her breath. Richard was still all right; he was hanging on.

"I favor the direct approach," J. B. whispered. "You?"

She nodded and together they walked into the dining room. "Hello, Vinnie," J. B. said cheerfully, the borrowed gun pointed at D'Amours. "Playing fair, I hope?"

Richard grinned broadly and blew Sheridan a kiss.

It occurred to her that he was having a grand time for himself.

Of the stone-faced school of poker players, Vinnie registered neither surprise nor indignation. "J. B.," he said, as if greeting a guest. His eyes fastened on Sheridan. "I told the boys they should have grabbed you when they had the chance."

"I think they knew better," Sheridan said cockily.

"Dumb move on my part, not nabbing you instead of J. B. St. Charles would've been more likely to make an even trade for his ladylove."

"Egad, Pop," Sheridan said, "Vinnie even talks like you."

"He was on the wrong side of the aisle at the same school," J. B. said.

Richard slowly fanned the cards in his hand. "You're wrong, Mr. D'Amours," he said, not raising his voice. "I wouldn't have traded even if Sheridan had been involved. I would have torn this place apart piece by piece. And you with it."

J. B. grinned. "I like a man with a sense of romance. By the way, you winning?"

"This is the decisive hand," Richard said.

"Well, don't let us stop you." J. B. waved his gun. "Play fair, now, Vinnie."

"Why? You're not going to let me walk away with that necklace," Vinnie hissed.

"Not the fake, no, but it looks to me like St. Charles here is betting one damned beauty of a genuine necklace. You wouldn't want to deny him a chance of win-

ning a few hundred grand off you, would you? Go on,
Vinnie. Play."

Sheridan groaned. "J. B., why are you encouraging
them?"

"Why not? We've got time."

Thirty minutes, to be exact. Sheridan nodded; he had
a point. If they could keep D'Amours occupied, there
was less of a chance of his coming up with some way
of extricating himself from his present predicament.
J. B. kept the gun pointed in Vinnie's general direction,
but Sheridan didn't think her father could shoot him.

"Dealer takes one," Vinnie said, and the game proceeded.

From the betting and the smug look on Richard's
face, Sheridan guessed he had a hell of a hand. She wandered over and stood behind him, but he wouldn't let
her see his cards. "Mustn't cheat," he said, a gleam in
his black eyes.

Finally Richard saw Vinnie's bet and called.

But Vinnie refused to show his hand right away. "I
didn't kill that girl," he said, almost in a whine. "I was
outside, in the car. I was desperate for money. You remember, J. B. I'd been on a losing streak for weeks back
then. I *had* to have cash."

"Someone else's?" Richard said coldly.

"At the time it didn't matter. I was hooked on gambling, lots worse than now, had a load of bad debts, the
wrong people crawling all over me for money. That
didn't change, even after that fiasco at the Livingston
house. All I had was that stupid bogus necklace. I wasn't

supposed to even have that. The guy who master-
minded the heist—"

"Bernard?" J. B. asked.

So he knew that, too, Sheridan thought.

"Yeah," Vinnie said, his voice sharp with bitterness,
"Bernard. He got rid of the junk, but I'd snatched that
fake necklace out from under his nose. I was a gambler.
I knew what I could do with a piece like that on a poker
table. I never figured on losing it, though."

"That's the thing about gambling," J. B. said, speaking with the voice of experience. "You never figure on
losing."

Vinnie looked up at his old nemesis. "How come you
waited twenty-five years to get even, J. B.?"

"In the first place, I never made the connection between the fake and the Livingston heist. I was busy
with other things at the time."

"Yeah. I remember your wife."

"In the second place," J. B. said, and Sheridan could
hear the weariness in his voice, "I had a daughter to
raise. I couldn't be settling old scores."

In her years as a private investigator, Sheridan had run
into dozens of people who had stepped across the line between right and wrong. Some knew what they were doing
and had no regrets; some knew what they were doing and
had regrets. Others simply had no idea there was any
such thing as right and wrong. Looking at Vinnie's face
as he clutched his poker hand, Sheridan knew he had
done wrong. But so did he. Not that he would have ad-
mitted as much if his hand hadn't been forced, so to speak.

"What about Bernard?" Sheridan asked. "Have you heard from him? Do you know where he is? It's possible, Vinnie, that the district attorney might work out a deal with you. You could turn state's evidence and give them Bernard."

Vinnie shook his head. "He'd kill me."

"Perhaps you should discuss this with the authorities," Richard said.

J. B. licked his lips. "Yeah, good idea. Vinnie, for God's sake, will you put down your cards?"

At that moment three men walked into the room. "Well, well, well," Richard said softly, and Sheridan, too, recognized them as the three who had attacked Richard on the yacht.

J. B. moved closer to D'Amours. "Call them off, Vinnie."

"I can't, they're not mine."

Sheridan's eyes met Richard's. "Bernard's men," they said simultaneously.

A dark heavyset man stepped forward. "No one needs to get hurt, but if anyone moves, the girl gets it first."

"Why is it always me?" Sheridan muttered. But she knew it was a small point: the men looked professional and ruthless. Once they had what they wanted, they would undoubtedly kill her, Richard and J. B. and maybe Vinnie, too.

The speaker of the trio jerked his gun at J. B. "Drop it, nice and easy."

Surreptitiously Sheridan glanced at her watch. In

three minutes Lieutenant Davis and his crew would arrive. She didn't want to be in a position to be taken hostage or killed in the cross fire or, for that matter, killed before the three minutes were up.

Apparently J. B.'s mind was operating in a similar vein. "No one has to get hurt here," he said, stepping behind Vinnie and sliding his gun to the floor.

Sheridan's eyes met Richard's, and she calmly willed him to know what she was thinking. *We have to be patient…we can't do anything rash….* Karate and judo had trained her mind as well as her body. She put into place the incredible self-discipline, the knowledge to know when to act…and when not to act. Until the three men moved within range, until they attacked, until they gave her the chance to disarm all three at once, there was simply nothing she could do…except be prepared for ten o'clock.

"You." The gun was waved at her now. "Get the necklaces and hand them to me."

Calmly Sheridan scooped up the two necklaces. "Think your boss'll be able to tell which is which this time?"

He didn't react: a professional.

"So you guys don't work for Vinnie," J. B. said. "Bernard's your man, huh? We stumbled into it this time, Sher."

Sheridan had no desire to move away from the table, Richard, J. B. or even Vinnie. They *had* to stay together. When the police arrived, she didn't want any one of them to be a handy hostage. She pretended her hands were shaking and dropped one of the necklaces on the table. The three thugs took one step forward. She smiled apologetically, scooping the necklace up again. "Sorry. I'm a bit jittery."

She saw Richard's eyebrow lift. It was a small gesture, but one that renewed her confidence.

"Yeah," the thug said. "Hand 'em over."

But it was ten o'clock. The police kicked open the door, and as they swooped into the room, J. B., Richard and Sheridan acted in unison and dove under the table. Being professionals, J. B. and Sheridan knew when to duck. Being Richard St. Charles, Richard knew Sheridan. A half second later Vinnie joined them.

Being professionals of a different sort, the three thugs knew when not to shoot. They lowered their guns and went quietly.

12

LATER, AFTER STATEMENTS to police and listening to their usual lectures on private investigators, the temporarily reunited partners of Weaver Investigations joined Richard St. Charles for a drink on his yacht in San Francisco Bay. The night air was brisk, but they sat on the deck under the stars, the three of them drinking Scotch. J. B. had already called Lucy and told her all was well.

"Well, St. Charles," J. B. said, settling back in his chair, "don't you want to know if you'd have won that hand?"

Richard smiled. He was sitting in a chair kitty-corner to J. B. while Sheridan was on the deck, leaning against his solid legs and dreaming dreams. "Doesn't make any difference to me," he said.

"How the hell could it not make any difference? You stood to lose three hundred grand! Sheridan, what kind of man have you got yourself mixed up with?"

"One who isn't a compulsive gambler," she replied.

"All right, St. Charles, what if I told you I grabbed Vinnie's hand before we left and have it right here in my pocket?"

"I'd believe you."

Sheridan swallowed a laugh.

"Would you want to set up a little game? You start fresh, I'll play Vinnie's hand. We'll see what happens."

Before Richard could reply, Sheridan shook her head. "No way, J. B. At this point another poker game would be completely gratuitous. The police have Vinnie, and they think he's going to lead them to Bernard and testify against him. The case is closed."

"Who the hell's talking about a damned case? This is *poker!*" J. B. wailed. "You used to like a good game every now and then, Sher, and don't you try to pretend otherwise."

Richard sipped his drink, a mildly amused look on his face. "She's turning into a stodgy financial analyst again right before our very eyes, J. B."

"Financial analysts are not necessarily stodgy. I'm just trying to be practical. For heaven's sake, Richard, don't you think you've had your fill of poker?"

"I don't know," he said, pressing his knees more firmly and sensuously against her. "It might be fun to see what Vinnie was betting on."

"That's my man," J. B. said.

"But I won't start fresh." Richard fished five cards out of his pocket. "I've got my hand here."

"You two are hopeless," Sheridan muttered.

"And look who's talking," her father said.

Richard rubbed her shoulders, prompting untold sensations to course through her body. "J. B. has a point. I don't think we're any more hopeless than a woman who wears a getup like that to take on a bunch of crooks."

J. B. chuckled. "No one's ever dared to tell her that, St. Charles. All these years I've been trying to tell her she can't go around looking like she's in her pajamas—"

"The *judogi* allows for freedom of movement," she said loftily, "which came in very handy tonight when I had to rescue you, J. B. And if I'd had to take on those three thugs—"

"That's my daughter," J. B. said, "Bruce Lee II. She poses as a bore in penny loafers, but underneath she's ready to leap into her pjs and take on a roomful of bad guys with guns."

"It's all coming back to me," Sheridan said, "why I left San Francisco."

J. B. reached over and patted her on the knee. "You did good tonight, kid." He turned to Richard. "Now about that hundred grand…"

"Water over the dam, J. B.—unless you'd like to wager it on Vinnie's hand?"

If Richard hadn't had his knees pressed against her shoulders, Sheridan would have leaped up. "No! J. B., you can't take that kind of risk."

"That is a little steep, St. Charles. I mean, if I lose the hand, you know I can't come up with that kind of cash. Besides, I don't owe you a dime."

"Fine," Richard said.

"Just like that?"

"Richard, he can't stand not knowing what's in your hand."

"I'd be glad to show it to him…."

"No," J. B. said. "This is too good…"

Sheridan regarded her father dubiously. "J. B., are you turning into a compulsive gambler?"

"All right, all right. Let's see what you got."

"If you'll recall," Richard said, his voice rough edged yet smooth, "I was the one who had called."

Muttering to himself, J. B. fished out the cards and turned them over on the table. A straight, king high. It was a good hand.

"Very nice." Richard turned his cards over one by one. "Seven of hearts," he said, "eight of hearts, nine of hearts, ten of hearts." He paused. "Jack of hearts."

Sheridan clapped her hands. "I don't believe it! Richard, you would have won!"

"I feel like I just saved myself a hundred grand. I— Hey, wait a minute. Wait just a minute, St. Charles! That's not a jack of hearts! That's a jack of diamonds!"

Richard peered at the cards. "So it is," he said, then leaned back and grinned at J. B. "But I can pretend, can't I?"

"I don't know about you, Sher," J. B. said, "but me, I'm going home."

"That's a good thought," Sheridan said. "Where have you been sleeping in the meantime?"

"Oh. Lucille offered me a bunk at her place."

"Lucille!"

Even Richard's eyes widened.

"Yeah, sure. You know Lucille. She likes to keep track of where I am."

"You mean she knew all along?" Sheridan asked.

"'Course. Not every detail, because, well, for heaven's

sake, do you know what my life would be like if I'd let that woman worry about me?"

"It's okay to let your daughter worry, but not your secretary. I can't believe she lied to me."

"Only because I told her to." J. B. patted her on the top of her head. "See you around, kid. It's going to feel good to sleep in a proper bed tonight."

It was Richard who pointed out, when J. B. had taken the launch back himself, that Sheridan had no way to get to the dock. "The launch service doesn't operate," he said, "at two-thirty in the morning."

IN THE SOFT GLOW OF DAWN they were lying side by side beneath the satin-covered down comforter on the giant bed in Richard's stateroom. The yacht seemed to undulate with them as they swayed in and out of sleep. It had been a long, long day. They had walked into the room with no intentions of making love until they had slept and digested all that had happened to them during the past few days. There had been no demands.

But there were desires, longings that had built throughout the afternoon and evening, so that their bodies had other plans. They needed release. They needed a few moments of abandonment.

No words were spoken. Responding to unconscious signals, they removed their clothes, letting them fall where they may. And they came together at once. Richard lifted her hips, lowered her onto him, and they fell onto the bed, already joined.

Again and again Sheridan had pulled him deeper

into her, wanting him to be like that always, a part of her, yet knowing that was impossible. He could never be a part of anyone. And neither could she.

In the stillness of the room, her body at last quiet, Sheridan willed herself to think and to speak. "I'm not going to hold you to what you told me earlier in the car," she said. "Adrenaline sometimes makes us say things we might regret later. Emotions tend to run high in a dangerous situation."

"Sheridan, don't patronize me." He didn't raise his voice. "I didn't say anything I would regret—ever."

"Richard, I'm not always the woman you've seen the past few days. Most of the time I'm—as J. B. so aptly put it—a bore in penny loafers. All I'm saying is, when our lives get back to normal, you don't have to love that woman. I'll understand." She licked her lips, cool and salty, tasting of him. "I'm returning to Boston tomorrow...today, actually. I have a job there, a life."

With his palm he touched the flatness of her stomach. He was the only man who had known both Sheridan Weavers. He had seen her in Boston; he had seen her in San Francisco. But it was the wild, brash San Francisco Sheridan he had claimed to have fallen in love with. She had long ago given up hope of finding a man who would love the two women she enjoyed being.

"I won't stop you from going back," he said.

"I understand."

"No, I don't think you do. I haven't changed my mind. I'm in love with you. I don't give a damn if you want to stay at United Commercial, or move back here and work with J. B., or start your own agency or go into something else altogether. None of that makes any difference to me. You have to live your own life, Sheridan. We both do. But I also want us to have a life together." He rolled onto his side and smiled into her eyes. "If you need to stay in Boston, I'll adjust. It's an interesting city."

She looked startled. "You mean you'd move out there?"

"Lock, stock and barrel, darlin'. I'm in the position to do as I damn well please, and I will. But not until you've decided whether or not you want to stay out there."

"I don't know what to say." She averted her eyes from the intensity and love in his. "Richard...I'm not sure I'm in love with you. No, no, that's not it. I know, deep down, that I love you more than I've ever imagined I could love anyone. You're everything I ever dreamed about. But I'm not sure I love you the way I'm supposed to love you."

He laughed softly. "I have no complaints."

"I don't mean physically! Lordy, we have no problems there." She grinned, remembering, but quickly grew serious again. "That's not what I'm talking about. Richard, you're an independent man—you're whole and vibrant and alive. I don't see you as the other half of myself. And I wonder if I should."

"Why in hell should I be the other half of you, or you be the other half of me? We're not arms and legs, sweet love, we're people. Together, we're a man and a woman who love each other, nothing more, nothing less. That alone is magical. But we're not a part of each other. I love you as you are, Sheridan, but you're not a part of me. I don't want that. And yet I can't imagine my life without you."

Her eyes filled with tears as she looked at him and touched his face. "I can't believe…that's exactly how I feel…it's wonderful, you're wonderful. Oh, Richard, I do love you!"

She hurled herself into his arms, and he caught her by the waist, rolling her on top of him, until his mouth found hers and they kissed madly, drinking in the joy and love and passion that was theirs. His hands smoothed from her buttocks, along her waist and up her back to her shoulder blades, leaving a trail of fire in their wake.

"We'll never get any sleep this way," she murmured.

"Good. I never want to sleep. I want to stay awake the rest of my life and make love to you."

She laughed. "Sounds wonderfully exhausting."

"Doesn't it, though?"

His thumbs fit under her breasts, and he lifted her torso off his chest, holding her aloft. "You're so beautiful. You look so healthy, so confident. There's nothing I'd change about you, love, nothing."

Slowly, slowly, he lowered her toward him, but stopped when the soft flesh of her breast reached his lips. She could feel the imprint of each of his fingers on her back, as if they were searing her flesh, stamping her not with his ownership, but with the passion and promise of his love.

She cried out his name, and finally, with delicious

precision, he brought the pink nipple into his mouth and teased it with his tongue, licking and stroking, until she was groaning with pleasure.

Then he lifted her higher, and his tongue and lips coursed down her stomach, the skin luminous and sensitive from their last bout of lovemaking, still alive, still ready to burn under the wet heat of his kiss. His hands slipped down to her waist, lifting her effortlessly and bringing her down in a rush of sensation, his tongue, lips and gentle teeth plunging into the dark center of her. Her flesh yielded to him. Her body throbbed with ecstasy.

Quickly, fiercely, lovingly, he grasped her hips and brought them down onto his, and himself into her. She simply held on for a moment lost in time, reveled in the fullness of him inside her, the hardness of his body, his masculinity, his sensitivity.

But their bodies soon demanded more, and he moved inside her, pulsing, turning her to liquid. Her senses were heightened, dominating, refusing to let her mind complete a conscious thought. Acutely attuned to the body dancing in union with hers, until at last tiny explosions rippled through them both, filling the dawn and their lives with the joy of love.

Afterward the room shone with the light of morning, and they slept.

ON THE THIRTIETH FLOOR of the United Commercial Insurance Building in downtown Boston, Donald Agnew was going over a stack of printouts at Sheridan's desk. His leather-bound appointment book was open beside him. He was wearing a tan chino suit and shiny tasseled loafers.

The telephone rang; he picked it up. "Donald Agnew.... No, no, you have the right extension. Ms Weaver is not in, but I'm sure I can help you." He swiveled in his chair, saw the dark-haired woman in the light-gray linen suit and black pumps and paled. "But perhaps you should call back in fifteen minutes. I'm sorry, it's impossible for me to talk now." He hung up and grinned sheepishly. "Sher."

"Hello, Donald," she said coolly.

"We didn't expect you back so soon."

He had her pull up a chair to her own desk, and they went over all that had happened since she had departed for San Francisco on the trail of her father. Which was precisely nothing.

United Commercial, it appeared, could function admirably without her. More to the point, so could Donald Agnew. But accustomed to the corporate hierarchy as he was, he cheerfully gathered up his belongings, left her with the printouts and shuffled off to his own windowless cubby.

With less relish than she had anticipated, Sheridan got back to work.

Richard had suggested she spend her first week back in Boston alone. "Pretend," he had said with a small smile, "that I don't exist." At the time Sheridan had appreciated his sensitivity and utter lack of possessiveness. Now she wasn't so sure. A week without Richard seemed interminable.

Nevertheless, after a few days she fell back into her old routines…but there were small differences. Instead of beginning the day with classical music and just enough time to get herself dressed and to the office by nine o'clock, she rose at five-thirty and hauled herself off to the dojo, the training hall in Kenmore Square where she practiced her judo and karate.

And at night, instead of relishing the quiet of her apartment and her aloneness, she often found herself sitting on her rooftop deck staring up at the sky, pretending she was on a yacht in San Francisco Bay.

Sheridan missed Richard more than she had ever imagined she would. She missed his arguments, his laughter, his lovemaking. And yet knowing he was coming to Boston when their week apart had ended made the missing bearable. Wherever she went, whatever she did, it was as if he were there with her. Stubborn and independent people though they were, somehow his spirit and hers were tangled up together, separate but inseparable.

On cool lonely nights in bed, she would force herself to imagine what she would do if he didn't return, and couldn't. On the surface her life had gotten back to its pre-Richard St. Charles normalcy—and she still wanted him. What about Richard, now that he was living without her "cockiness"?

She needn't have worried. On Sunday night his plane landed at Logan Airport, and he sauntered off wearing a charcoal worsted suit with a white button-down shirt, a regimental striped tie and cordovan wing-tip shoes. His hair was neatly trimmed and brushed.

If it weren't for the black eyes and roguish grin, Sheridan might not have recognized him.

"Hello, love," he said in his sandpaper-and-silk voice. "You look dazzling."

One night after work she had stopped at a boutique on Newbury Street and picked up a pair of slim crop pants and a flowered chintz shirt.

"Thank you. I...you..."

He grinned. "Think I'll pass as a proper Boston executive?"

"I think so. But why would you want to?"

"Why, love, to preserve your reputation, of course."

"You're having a grand time for yourself, aren't you?"

"Just being with you again is grand, Sheridan," he murmured.

He refused her offer to stay in her apartment—once again, to preserve her reputation—and installed himself at the Ritz, in an elegant room overlooking the Public Gardens. They made love on the big bed and afterward ordered room service.

In the ensuing days Richard insinuated himself neatly into her routines and revealed an extensive wardrobe of preppy clothes. Every minute she wasn't working they spent together; he also turned up at the office every day to join her for lunch. No matter how inconspicuous he tried to be, his presence in the halls of United Commercial prompted excited questions. Always Sheridan explained him away as "my friend, Richard St. Charles, from San Francisco." Of course, that was never good enough. Curious stares followed them.

One night at the Ritz Sheridan caught him pulling pricetags off a Brooks Brothers shirt. "What are you doing?"

"What does it look like?" he countered patiently.

"But that's a new shirt."

"Yes, it is."

"I thought—They're all new, aren't they? The shirts, the shoes, the suits. You didn't own anything like that until you met me."

He smiled. "No, actually I did, in the old days. I was the king of the pinstripes. Don't you like the new me?"

"I like *you*, Richard. I don't care if you wear pin-stripes or T-shirts. But don't pretend to be someone you're not."

"Ah, now we're getting somewhere."

She sighed. "Those sound like your words to me, right?"

"As I said when I first met you, we all have our ruses. I want us to be together, Sheridan. I don't care how."

"But not at the risk of denying who you are!"

"Why not?" he queried, his eyes alert. "Isn't that what you're doing?"

She began to shake. "Then you don't like my life in Boston. You never intended to stay here. You just want to show me how dull and boring I am. Well, you've done a fine job of it! You're a terrific caricature of me and my friends. Has it been amusing, Mr. St. Charles? I hope it has. Because I'll tell you right now, the Sheridan Weaver you've been seeing the past two weeks *is the real me*."

"I never doubted that for a moment," he said steadily, "but is she doing what she really wants to do with her life?"

She snatched the shirt off the bed and threw it at him. "If you hurry, you can get to Brooks Brothers in time to return this. But don't say I didn't warn you, Richard. When the adrenaline rush ended, I started looking like an ordinary businesswoman, didn't I?"

"No, as a matter of fact, you didn't—which, I suppose, is half the problem, isn't it? Why do you persist in *acting* like an ordinary businesswoman?"

"What do you suggest I act like? Come, tell me, Mr. St. Charles. You know so much about me. Who am I?"

"Sheridan, please. Don't be upset. I didn't mean to imply—"

"Dammit, don't you see? I can't go back to San Francisco and be an extension of you! But I don't want you to stay here and be an extension of me." Her eyes filled with tears, which she brushed away angrily. "It's impossible, isn't it? There's just no answer."

She turned on her heels and walked out. Richard, stonily silent, didn't follow.

FOR TWO DAYS Sheridan put in long hours at U. C. and the dojo. In some ways the work and exercise were a substitute for the sex she had had with Richard. They left her mind and body numb, and because there was no choice, she could sleep without agonizing over the loss of the solid male body beside her, in her.

In other ways her mind and body knew they were being duped, that no amount of work or exercise could replace the hours she and Richard had spent exploring and satiating each other's body and spirit.

And in all ways the work and exercise were never a substitute for the love she had for Richard. She missed his laughter, his companionship, even his anger.

Dammit, she thought, slamming her pencil down on her desk, why had he given in so easily? Why had she stormed out when all they had needed to do was talk?

Talk, talk, talk. They could talk forever and never come up with a solution. He wanted his old Sheridan Weaver back. But his old Sheridan Weaver had never existed.

Or maybe she was deluding herself? How else could she explain her rekindled interest in the martial arts? Even when she and Richard had been on more intimate terms, she had taken time for her workouts while he would go running on the banks of the Charles River. If she wasn't deluding herself, how did she explain her insidious boredom with the world of insurance? Her job hadn't changed in the course of a month. There were the usual problems and personalities to deal with—even if they didn't seem to hold the challenge that chasing down a missing father had.

Yet it seemed as if she had no real choices. Remaining for the rest of her career in a thirtieth-floor cubby with a window didn't intrigue her. But neither did watering roses on Russian Hill for the rest of her life. Somehow she wanted both her worlds to come together.

A shadow fell across her desk.

"Agnew," she said irritably, "I'm not in the mood. Get the hell out of my light."

"Ms Weaver?"

The voice was not Donald Agnew's, but this time around she recognized it. Her head shot up. "Richard!"

He was wearing a T-shirt and natural linen pants. "Ms Weaver," he said formally, "my name is Richard St. Charles. I'm a friend of your father's, Jorgensen Beaumont Weaver. He suggested I come to you with my problem."

"Richard, please…"

"You see, I have an extremely ticklish problem. A few weeks ago I purchased a diamond and emerald necklace from the Livingston collection for three hundred thousand dollars. During the past month or so, your father and I have become friends. He asked if he could borrow the necklace for one night, and I agreed."

"You're making this up, aren't you? You wouldn't really lend J. B. a necklace worth three hundred thousand?"

"I did, Sheridan."

"Oh, good God." She opened up her right-hand drawer, dragged out the familiar amber bottle and poured herself a spoonful of the white liquid. "Maalox…ulcer acting up, first time in weeks."

"Nine-to-five schedules will do that to you. Shall I continue?" He straightened, still pretending that he didn't know her. "Apparently he used the necklace in his proposal of marriage to his secretary, Lucille Stein. He wanted her to wear it on their wedding day."

"Argh!" She pressed one forearm against her stomach and held up a hand. "It's okay, I'm all right. Just go on…please."

"Lucille—Ms Stein—thought J. B. was playing a cruel joke on her. She said she'd loved him for all these years, and now he didn't respect her any more than to stick a paste necklace under her nose and pretend to want to marry her. How could he toy with her feelings that way, who was she but the woman who'd helped him out of so many scrapes, et cetera, et cetera. She was, he says, incredibly furious. He tried to explain that he was serious, but she insisted he wasn't, grabbed the necklace and stalked out."

"She grabbed the necklace!"

Richard nodded grimly, and suddenly Sheridan knew he wasn't fabricating some tale. "J. B. tried to follow her, but she'd learned a few tricks from him over the years and managed to disappear."

"Poor Lucy. I had no idea…."

"Poor Lucy! That woman has *my* necklace!"

"Mr. St. Charles, you like to live dangerously, don't you? Tell me, what do you want me to do?"

"Recover the necklace. Since it's a salvage job, I'm prepared to pay you half its value."

One hundred and fifty thousand dollars. Sheridan could live a long time on that kind of money. Or she could invest it. In one of Richard's horses, say. Or anything. She liked the possibilities. She liked the risks. She could feel her worlds uniting. She could be an MBA and an investigator. Life didn't have to be rigid. She could have her adventures, her independence, her routines. "Do you have any clue as to where she might be?" she asked.

Richard hesitated. "J. B. thinks she might have gotten herself into a high-stakes game with a few 'sleazes,' as Lucille might call them, and is going to gamble the necklace."

"Thinking it's a fake."

"Yes."

"Egad."

"He says you'll have a better chance of tracking her down because you're not as emotionally involved."

"She's been like a second mother to me!"

"But she's a woman to him. There's a difference."

The warmth in his voice drew her eyes to his, and she saw warmth there, too, and love and caring. Nothing had changed. She could see all the possibilities of a life with him. Without him life didn't exist, not for her. "Yes," she said, "there is a difference. I'll take the case, Mr. St. Charles. But you'll have to give me a few minutes. I have to type a letter of resignation."

"Sheridan…"

There was an edge of panic to his voice. She grinned up at him, her eyes big and round and filled with energy. "I'm sure, Richard. Very sure."

THEY RESCUED LUCILLE and the necklace from a gang of thieves off the coast of Hawaii. She was miffed at her own impulsiveness, but otherwise undaunted by the experience. "Guess I don't want to live J. B.'s life, after all," she said when she was safely aboard Richard's yacht. "It's much easier just to answer telephones—plenty of excitement for me. I can't believe the old buzzard was serious. Hmm. Hope he hasn't rescinded his offer."

Since she hadn't cost him three hundred thousand, after all, Richard and Sheridan assured her that he probably hadn't. Lucille went happily below, planning which shade of blond she'd dye her hair for the wedding.

"I have a mad urge," Richard said as they basked in the glorious Hawaiian sunshine, "to pitch that damned necklace into the ocean."

"What! It's worth—"

"Three hundred thousand. Yes, believe me, I know. But how much have I dropped on it already?"

"Well, it depends if you count the hundred thousand you lost to win the fake."

"I count it."

"That's one hundred, plus the three hundred you paid for the real thing, plus various and sundry expenses amounting to Lord knows what to lose it and get it back and...I guess you've dropped a lot."

"I guess." He crawled over and sat beside her on the deck. "But it would probably be found by some scoundrel if I toss it."

"Are you going to let Lucille wear it for her wedding?"

"Oh, you didn't hear that part, did you? She doesn't like it. Thinks it's gaudy and weighs too much. This, mind you, from a woman who still wears her hair like

Marilyn Monroe. I believe she said she would just as soon get her jewelry at Woolworth's. Although she appreciates J. B.'s sentiment, wearing my necklace, said she, would give her heart failure."

Sheridan laughed. "Isn't she wonderful?"

"In her own way, yes, she is. She doesn't play to anyone else's tune—like her future stepdaughter." He smiled, moving closer. "I've been imagining how all those diamonds and emeralds would look reflected in your eyes. You're a beautiful woman, Sheridan. You could walk down the aisle in a *judogi*, or whatever you call that thing, and I don't think anyone would pay any attention."

"I could, could I? What aisle is this?"

"A figurative one. I always thought we'd be married on the yacht."

Not "my" yacht, she noted, just "the" yacht. It made a difference. She smiled, the tenderness in her heart reaching her eyes. "That's what I've always thought, too."

"Then—"

"I'll marry you, yes, and I'll wear the necklace and hope all who see the sparkle in my eyes know it's inspired by you, not the jewels. You're my light, Richard, my love, my joy. I love you."

"We're just beginning, love, you know that, don't you?"

Her face lit up with the anticipation of the times they had ahead of them together—the adventures, the lovemaking, the fights, the peace, the happiness. And this wasn't a dream. This wasn't a silly fantasy. It was their reality. Their life together would be wonderful.

Sheridan drew herself to him and kissed him lightly, lovingly. "Our life together will always be just beginning."

He held her face in his hands and smiled, saying nothing, for nothing needed to be said.

We hope you enjoyed reading

CAPTIVATED
by
CARLA
NEGGERS

Look for six new
steamy romances
each and every month
from Harlequin® Blaze™.

Red-Hot Reads.

Choose the romance that suits your reading mood

Passion

Harlequin Presents®
Intense and provocatively
passionate love affairs set
in glamorous international
settings.

Silhouette Desire®
Rich, powerful heroes and
scandalous family sagas.

Harlequin® Blaze™
Fun, flirtatious and steamy
books that tell it like it is,
inside and outside the
bedroom.

In 2009 Harlequin celebrates
60 years of pure reading pleasure!

We're marking this occasion by offering
16 **FREE** full books to download and read.

We invite you to visit and share the Web site
with your friends, family
and anyone who enjoys reading.

THE HARLEQUIN FAMOUS FIRSTS COLLECTION™

WE HOPE YOU ENJOYED THIS TITLE FROM THE HARLEQUIN FAMOUS FIRSTS COLLECTION™.

DISCOVER MORE GREAT ROMANCES FROM HARLEQUIN® AND SILHOUETTE® BOOKS.

Whether you prefer romantic suspense, heartwarming or passionate novels, each and every month Harlequin® and Silhouette® have new books for you!

AVAILABLE WHEREVER YOU BUY BOOKS.

Use the coupon below and save $1.00 on the purchase of any Harlequin® or Silhouette® series-romance book!

THE HARLEQUIN FAMOUS FIRSTS COLLECTION™

WE HOPE YOU ENJOYED THIS TITLE
FROM THE HARLEQUIN
FAMOUS FIRSTS COLLECTION™.

DISCOVER MORE GREAT ROMANCES FROM HARLEQUIN® AND SILHOUETTE® BOOKS.

Whether you prefer romantic suspense, heartwarming or passionate novels, each and every month Harlequin® and Silhouette® have new books for you!

AVAILABLE WHEREVER YOU BUY BOOKS.

Use the coupon below and save $1.00 on the purchase of any Harlequin® or Silhouette® series-romance book!

$1.⁰⁰ OFF the purchase of any Harlequin® or Silhouette® series-romance book.

Coupon valid until March 31, 2010. Redeemable at participating retail outlets in Canada only. Limit one coupon per customer.

52608588

FFCDNCPN

THE HARLEQUIN FAMOUS FIRSTS COLLECTION™

THIS LIMITED-EDITION 12-BOOK
COLLECTION FEATURES SOME OF
THE FIRST HARLEQUIN® BOOKS BY
NEW YORK TIMES BESTSELLING
AUTHORS OF TODAY!

Available March:
The Matchmakers by Debbie Macomber
Tangled Lies by Anne Stuart
Moontide by Stella Cameron
Tears of the Renegade by Linda Howard

Available June:
State Secrets by Linda Lael Miller
Uneasy Alliance by Jayne Ann Krentz
Night Moves by Heather Graham
Impetuous by Lori Foster

Available September:
The Cowboy and the Lady by Diana Palmer
Fit To Be Tied by Joan Johnston
Captivated by Carla Neggers
Bronze Mystique by Barbara Delinsky

Available wherever books are sold.

Each and every month, discover new romances from Harlequin and Silhouette Books, and the Love Inspired series.

PASSION

HARLEQUIN *Presents* · Silhouette *Desire*

HARLEQUIN *Blaze*

HOME & FAMILY

HARLEQUIN *American ★ Romance* · Silhouette SPECIAL EDITION

HARLEQUIN *Super Romance*

ROMANCE

HARLEQUIN *Romance* · Harlequin® Historical
Historical Romantic Adventure!

SUSPENSE & PARANORMAL

HARLEQUIN INTRIGUE · Silhouette Romantic SUSPENSE

Silhouette nocturne

INSPIRATIONAL ROMANCE

Love Inspired · *Love Inspired* SUSPENSE

Love Inspired HISTORICAL

Available wherever you buy books.

www.eHarlequin.com

NYTBPA4R2